SHANE DOS

for Elma

With thanks to Arno, Boguś, Mike, Charlie, Martin and anyone that I may have forgotten.

SHANE DOS

Tim Orchard

fiction direct

FICTION DIRECT

Shane Dos

First published in Great Britain by Fiction Direct 2009

Copyright © Tim Orchard 2009

ISBN: 978-0-9555503-1-7

British Library Cataloguing-in-Publication Data
A catalogue record for this book is available from the
British Library

Set in Garamond

Printed and bound in Great Britain by
Athenaeum Press Ltd., Gateshead, Tyne & Wear

Fiction Direct
20 Brockwell Court
Effra Road
Brixton, London SW2 1NA

www.fictiondirect.com

∽ 1 ∽

The room was stuffy, full of old dark furniture and smelt of sickness. The metal roller blinds outside the window were pulled halfway down to cut out the worst of the early morning sun. The old lady in the bed was propped into a sitting position with a couple of pillows. The yellow skin of her face was pulled tight on the bones and the remains of her grey hair scraped straight back over her skull and held with a clip. The framed photographs on the dressers and walls showed a vibrant smiling woman with various family and friends and bore absolutely no resemblance to the shrunken, dying person beneath the sheets.

This was their second visit. The first had been late afternoon the previous day. Her maid, who seemed to double as her nurse and companion told them, by that time of the day the drugs for the cancer left her almost comatose. Lola though, smiling and sad at the same time, had insisted. She shmoozed the maid, who herself must have been knocking seventy. She said. "I just want to sit with her. We've come all the way from England. It could be the last chance for me to see my great aunty and for her to see me. I am the last in the family now. What harm can it do, eh? Please."

Shane and Rob had sat for half an hour in an atmosphere that made them never want to grow old, while Lola held the ancient birds hand and tried to get some sense out of her. But the beloved aunty had just drifted in and out of consciousness. She barely recognized Lola, rambling sometimes, snoozing at others. At one point, Rob said to Lola. "Come on lovely, how much longer? This is doing my nut in." At the sound of his voice *Bis* (great) aunty opened her eyes wide, a smile came to her gummy gob and she said, clearly. *"El Inglés"* Then the morphine took over again and her eyelids fluttered shut.

As they walked down the apartment block stairs and out into the Madrid sun, Lola railed, in English. "The bitch! She must not die! Not yet! That would put the cat among the pigeons. Truly. She is the last of our family. For years in Spain no one talks about that time. Even my father whose parents lost everything didn't say a word." Lola gave a sick laugh. "And they were on the winning side. I ask him and he tells me the same as his parents told him. Don't talk about it. *Silencio*. What am I a *limón*? Don't I have a brain! Bah! Tomorrow we come back in the morning. Then, then we will see." Rob said. "Let's get a beer, that fucking bedroom gave me the creeps."

They sat outside a bar, under a red and white umbrella and drank a couple of *cervezas* while Lola calmed down. Shane spoke to Lola in Spanish, he said. "Do you really believe she'll be able to remember? Sixty years is a long time. Why didn't any of the family try to do something about it? See if it was still there or something." Lola gave a big sigh and shrugged, she said. "Fear? Just because the fighting stops things don't go back to normal. Not for a long time. People forget we have only been a democracy for thirty years. I don't think a lot of the old people thought it would even last this long. Perhaps if my parents had lived, it would be different now." Shane said. "What did happen to them?" She said. "Car crash, I was seventeen. I was left nothing." Shane said. "How old are you now?" Lola smiled and looked at him from under her eyelashes, she said. "Twenty three." She paused, smiled a bit more and said. "You're different to how he said you were." Now Shane smiled. Rob had an arm in the air with three fingers up as he tried to get the waiters attention for more beer, he said. "For fuck sake guys, English please! I'm starting to feel lonely here." Shane said. "I was asking about the old lady." Rob, tall and skinny was slumped back in his chair. Long white legs in baggy shorts stretched out in front of him, glimmering in the bright light, like fresh paint. Sunglasses sat up on the top of his head and his hair was tied back in a ponytail. He was pasty faced, with a fat nose and he looked like what he was. English.

To Lola, he said. "Yeh, Lola my lovely. That old bird, she don't seem capable of nothing, know what I mean? And what about that maid? Scary! Looks like that fucking dead actor, you know, the horror guy, Bela Lugosi." Lola laughed and said. "She's been with her forever, honey, ever since I was a little one." The beers came. Rob said. "Cheers mate." The waiter flared his nostrils, half closed his eyes and walked away without acknowledging him. Rob said. "Fuck sake! What's up with him!" Both Lola and Shane laughed and Rob said. "What? Anyway, what do you reckon? The maid and the old aunty, lesbians or what?" They giggled together, then Lola showed the steel in her character that belied the honeys and sweeties she lavished on Rob. "That old bitch spent everything on herself while the rest of the family struggled and tomorrow I'm going to make her pay. She has kept her secrets, now she tells me or it will be the worse for her." Shane and Rob looked at each other with raised eyebrows. Rob though was pleased with his lovely, and said to

Shane. "Told you she was tough, didn't I?"

So for the second visit they had arrived a little after nine am, Lola bristling with determination. The old girl may have been dying but at least this time she was awake, because she nodded at Shane and Rob as they entered. Lola sat beside the bed and held the old bird's hand, just the way she had the previous afternoon. Aunty was pleased to see whoever because nobody ever came. Lola was all solicitude asking questions about her illness like she really cared. Then there was some small talk with Lola gradually edging in on the main agenda and grande aunty talking about times long ago like it was yesterday. Every once in a while Rob would say to Shane. "What they saying now?" Shane took it all in, listened attentively because of Lola and because boredom had played him these cards and he thought he could smell the money. Whenever Rob asked him a question, Shane pulled a pained face and said. "They're just talking about the family and shit." And most of the time it was true. But slowly they were getting down to the nitty-gritty.

Lola began to insist there was something aunty wasn't telling her but the old girl played dumb. She got out her pocket book, carefully took out a photo and held it up to aunty. The old girl scrutinized the picture, laughed and shaking and wheezing said. "Did that come from your father? We, the children were all given one. It was supposed to be our legacy. My brother, your father's father also. This was his copy. He would naturally have given it to his son, your father. But it is nothing, it is fools gold my dear. This photograph is supposed to tell us where the family fortune was hidden but you can't even see who's who. I was there when this was taken. I was a teenager then but it means nothing to me now. Ask yourself why would there still be anything there? The place was burnt down. Do you think the Republican scum who did that would have left anything for us? Do you not think I've thought about it? My mother and father were murdered! And all the trouble we lived through? Perhaps it is all best forgotten." Lola still had hold of the old woman's hand and slowly she tightened her grip. Over Shane's shoulder, Rob said. "Don't look like Lola's getting what she wants." Lola squeezed, she said. "Don't bother with all of that, aunty. I know you are the only person left who knows exactly where this place was. You've refused to tell anybody all these years, claiming you couldn't remember because of the trauma. I don't believe you. I never believed you. You spent all the family's money. Look at you even now spending the last of it. No surprise you don't want to remember anything. But I want you to remember - for me."

The complete pain of her situation didn't seem to be reaching aunty through the residue of the night's morphine. Instead of crying out, she rallied and pulled herself up in the bed. She pursed her lips like she was drinking piss and said. "My god, I've had this for my whole life! Always the arguments. The money I've spent was left to me. It was mine! Now let go of my hand!" But Lola didn't let go. She eased off and said, quietly. "I don't want any of your money." She waggled the photo. "I just want to know where this is." The old lady sighed like she'd had enough and said. "Extremadura." Even Rob understood that bit of Spanish and whispered to Shane. "Fuck me, we already know that." To Rob and Shane, Lola said, sharply. "Wait outside."

They sat in the spotless kitchen and the maid made them coffee in tiny cups. Shane said. "What did Lola do in England?" Rob scratched his chin like it was a million years ago, he said. "What? Before she met me?" Shane nodded. Rob was someone he'd known under certain circumstances. They had done business together or rather Rob had done business for Shane. Now here he was out of the blue and determined in a way Shane would never have thought him capable of. Now he was a man with a plan, and Lola on his arm. Shane couldn't figure it. Couldn't figure how they worked together or what kind of a squib Lola had put up his arse to make him brave enough to get out of the debt people like Shane had shackled him with.

Rob said. "Old peoples homes, yeh, she was a carer." Shane thought of the way Lola had held the old dear's hand and said. "Poor fuckers." Rob did a double take, he said. "Come on man, she's just trying to do her best, you shouldn't talk about her like that." A couple of minutes later Lola came into the kitchen. Her eyes were hard and a flush lay under her sallow skin. She took Rob's hand the way lovers do and all business-like, said. "Okey dokey, come on honey, time to go."

Shane went back to his hotel, leaving Lola and Rob to rent a vehicle. He lay on the bed and wondered what to do. Was it worth risking his safety? They didn't know where he was staying and had he wanted to, this would have been the perfect time to disappear. He'd come to Madrid almost a couple weeks before, driven by cabin fever, boredom and need. He'd spent the time clubbing, drinking, throwing shapes at the beautiful women and seeing sights he'd already seen.

Outside of his home and the local village, he only felt safe in cities like Barcelona, Granada and Madrid, surrounded by millions of humans he didn't know and who didn't notice him. It was a choice he'd made. Sometimes he was lonely for the friends and people he knew and the heads that knew him too, but even after four years, to certain, types he was still like cash on the hoof. Yet nomatter how long he was away from England, however distant he cast himself from the past, he couldn't help expecting, at least unconsciously, to be discovered. Yet when it had happened it was a shock and completely different to anything he'd imagined.

It was late evening and Shane was sitting outside a small bar, a few hundred metres from his hotel. He was eating *patatas bravas* and drinking beer and watching the world go by. Thinking about going home the next day and thinking about what he was going to do that night. The bar was on the corner of a large paved square, busy with the comings and goings of a city heading out for the night. He noticed Lola first. She came out of the strollers slim and straight up. Her short dark hair was picked out at the tips in bright red and she had the face for it. She was slim in a blue and white, fifties-style blouse that almost came down to her midriff and had a nifty little stand-up collar. Her skirt was of some stretchy material. It was short and had the face of some Indian god or the other on it in pale washed out colours. She had good legs. Straight off Shane wanted to touch her. He didn't even notice the guy half a step behind her. Anyway wasn't she smiling at him - just a little bit, like she'd clocked him clocking her? Then some guy with white legs and trainers was in front of her and he was wearing shite shorts and a stupid baggy vest, with the name of some baseball team on it. One of his skinny arms was already outstretched and he was going. "Mate! Mate! You don't fucking know how happy I am to see you!" As well as knowing the gangly cunt coming full speed towards him and trying to decide whether he wanted to be found or just to fuck off or what. Shane noticed that the woman was hand in hand with the cunt and then Rob was on him, trying to hug him like they were long lost brothers. Half standing, Shane shoved him away and said. "Get the fuck off me!"

Rob laughed in a nervous, overexcited way and pulling out a chair flopped into it uninvited. The woman stood behind him with her hands on his shoulders like a Victorian matriarch. She was looking at Shane and looking at her, he said to Rob. "What are you doing here?" Rob made movements with his hands and hunched his neck down into his shoulders. "I'm here with -." He reached behind him and taking the woman by the forearm, drew her around beside him. "Er, this is Lola. Lola this is Shane." Shane made a move to rise but Lola smiled and leaning forward kissed him on both cheeks, before sitting in the chair next to him. Shane didn't know what to do. His mouth was dry and he could feel his heart trip hopping around in his chest. Rob said. "How about a drink? Fucking hell, fancy fucking meeting you, just like that! We've only been here a couple of days and the language is sending me fucking mental." He smiled at Lola as though it was her fault. "Once she starts giving it the old fucking Spanish, I can't understand a word she's on about."

Lola looked even better close up and Shane had to look away when she reached across the table and taking one of Rob's hands, said in good but idiomatic English. "Fuck a duck sweetie, it is Spain, I'm Spanish. Someone's got to do the talking or we'll both be up the old shit creek, darling." Shane couldn't help laughing. He looked at Rob and Rob smiled a stupid love stuck smile back at him, shrugged and said. "We met clubbing. Well, she was clubbing, I was - well, you know." Lola looked straight at Shane and smiled a clean open smile while her brown eyes held his in ambiguity. A waitress came over, they got drinks and Lola complimented Shane on his Spanish.

When they started a conversation in Spanish, Rob interrupted. "See, we're here on like family stuff. Fucking hell it's amazing. Wait while I fucking tell you, right!" Lola said. "Wait sweetie, wait. Shane doesn't want to hear all that family stuff." Rob shook his head and moved his hands like he was doing the hand-jive, he said. "No, lovely, see what I reckon is, I can't fucking do this if I don't know what the fuck is going on. It's like I been here two days and I've lost the fucking will to live, know what I mean? I go out to buy something and everywhere's shut. Fuck sake, what am I, some fucking dill that just stands around?" Lola paid Rob the compliment of listening to him and then taking a swig of her beer, said. "Aren't you happy you've met your old friend, honey? Why not forget my family and Spanish and speak English. Look, here we are, we're ships passing in the night darling, you, me, Shane. Let's just enjoy ourselves. Bugger *cerveza*, sorry lovely, I mean beer. Let's get something with a bit of bite. Well, what about it sweetie?" Somehow everything was alright when Lola said it was alright even if it was bullshit and Shane could see that. It didn't stop the half lob he had on from just sitting watching her.

2

While he'd been living in Spain, Shane had attempted to change himself. He had worked hard on his
Spanish. Even the Spanish did not recognize him as
English anymore, most of the time. His hair was
longer but neat rather than long and lightened to
almost blond by the sun. He had a smeggy, artist
type beard trimmed to his chin and a tan that
looked lived in. He tended to wear soft, good qual-
ity shirts and baggy linen trousers but he drew the
line at draping a jumper over his shoulders. The
way Shane saw it you could go too continental.
People took him for Scandinavian, German, whatever. Once when he was in Italy they had even
thought he was northern Spanish. It worked for
him, freed him sometimes from his past. Unlike
others, Shane didn't go to the coast. Didn't see, go
near or associate with anyone who would know

him and there were plenty who would and plenty ready to sell him to keep their own liberty. He was known. Killing cops don't make you a favourite with anybody. Fuck that. Loneliness is being a bit sad about yourself and your shit, dead is being dead.

Back in the day before day when he was still coming up, doing good and making plenty, people kept coming and going to Spain. Talking cheap property, sun, sea, blah,blah. It sounded good because money has to go somewhere, doesn't it? And doesn't everyone need somewhere they can escape to? The first time Shane came to Spain alone was on business, early in eighty-nine. Some fool needed topping and it was easy money for Shane. Even though he should have known better, what amazed him was that some people not only knew he was there, but why he was there. Crim's talk and not just to each other. They love to tell stories of what they did and what they know. He looked around and what he saw was somewhere where everybody seemed to know everybody else's runnings, like some little London. The coast didn't seem like much of a place to escape to.

After he'd completed, he rented a car and headed inland. Only then did Spain become real to him. The vastness of the country blew him away. He spent a couple of weeks all on his old oddy knocky, exploring Andalucia and Extremadura. Driving up around El Chorro there were lakes bigger than he'd ever seen in his life and little mountain roads that climbed up around them to high, empty plateaus of stone and scrub grass. In Extremadura there were woods as well as mountains, and rivers. It was beautiful. There was a half-arsed town called Albuquerque, where he stopped simply because the name held resonance.

He walked around the town and then sat at the bar and ate a *ración* of bean and pork stew and drank a beer. That single *cerveza* turned into huge, unexpected, rolling drunk of a day and night. Somehow as he ate the bar filled with people talking and eating and drinking. Beside him on a high stool at the bar was a guy his own age. Maybe it was Shane's phrase book on the counter or the fact that as the bar filled they seemed to get pushed closer together. Elbow to elbow they exchanged nods and grins. It turned out his name was Jesus. When Jesus was getting another beer, he nodded at Shane and fingered the bar bloke for two more. And so it went. Between Shane's pathetic few words of Spanish, Jesus's badly broken English and the phrase book, they communicated by eyebrows and eyes, back slaps and laughter. They roamed around the town together from bar to bar, from *cerveza* to J&B, like old mates. Later in the afternoon when the town started to draw its shutters for a bit of a snooze, they went to Jesus's apartment and smoked some lovely crumbly Zero Zero.

Jesus came from Malaga. When Shane asked him what he did for a living, he made vague gestures with his hands and crunched up his face like there were so many things, to name just one would not be fair. He'd left Malaga to get away from things, whatever. Shane began to laugh and Jesus did too. They high five'd each other and laughed, knowing it didn't matter. Albuquerque was quiet and cheap. There wasn't an exact answer. He shrugged and going to the fridge came back with two cold bottles. Yeh, he knew he'd have to go back sometime but not right now and they clanked bottles and laughed. Later they went out and hit the bars. Mad on good hash and J&B they talked nonsense and laughed for hours.

Shane awoke the next morning on the couch, fully dressed and covered in a velour curtain. Half his memory was wiped and his mouth wasn't just dry but dry and lumpy. The plastic carrier of puke beside the couch explained the lumps at least. Later Jesus explained with hand and face movements, how he'd hung the bag off Shane's ears to cut down on mess. Later again, when Jesus told Shane what he had paid for the apartment and they had managed to convert it back into real money, Shane looked around disbelievingly. It was huge with several rooms and an ancient bathroom all opening onto the fan shaped main room.

Okay, it was old and run down, above a flyblown shop that sold women's fashions that dated back to the seventies and shit but Jesus had paid less than eight grand for it only a year before. It was so far away from the flash villas on the coast, so absolutely nowhere, it really was an escape. Shane said. "If you ever want to, ah what is it? To *vender*?" Shane made hand movements like he was paying out money. "Get it?" Jesus got it. He made more hand movements that encompassed the whole flat and said. "Yeh, sure *hombre*." They smoked some more hash and strangely, kept in touch when Shane went back to England.

Jesus never did want to sell his place but one day he sent Shane a photograph. It was a house maybe forty K's from Albuquerque, just outside the village of Lugar de la Buja, on the edge of the Sierra de San Pedro. There was a piece of land and a couple of outbuildings. The house was old, with little windows and a tiled roof. An electricity cable looped up from a pylon by the road and a standpipe came up by the front door. On the back of the snap Jesus had scrawled a price of 10,000,000 Pesetas. From what Shane remembered, that was about ten grand. He put about twenty in a body belt and flew out. Jesus got hold of a notary and Shane gave his friend power of attorney and that was more or less it. In two or three months he was a property owner. Nobody back home knew a thing.

Over the next couple of years he went over to stay with Jesus whenever he had the time. Builders were organized and while the outside of the house remained almost the same, the inside was gutted, opened out and moderniz,ed. At the time, Shane didn't have a plan, didn't have an idea that he was preparing the future or even how near that future was.

Lola ordered Mojito's, a cocktail of rum, lime and mint, with brown sugar and lemonade. After two, Rob rummaged in the pocket of his shorts and pulled out a small round tin packed with little fella's and they necked one each. It was the first E Shane had had since leaving England and merely the bitter taste of it in the back of his throat made him feel good. He said. "You still at it?" Rob was emphatic. "No mate I told you, everything's different now. I've left that behind me. These are just for pleasure." Shane didn't believe him and told him so. Rob said. "Fuck it, that's the trouble with the world, people never want you to change. But this thing with Lola and me, it alters everything and I ain't going back. Look at you. You got away clean. No fucker knows where you went and let's face it, you were fucking public fucking enemy number fucking *uno* there for a while." He held out his hands in supplication. "Am I right or am I fucking right?" Before Shane could answer, Lola said. "Blimey darling, let's not get multilingual now! It's public fucking enemy number one or nothing." Rob kissed her. Shane wanted to kiss her. The waiter came with more drinks.

Shane didn't want to get into the past with Rob, didn't want to tell him anything about the last four years or even anything about yesterday. Fact was he didn't care if some cunt came along and put salt on Rob's tale and he curled up and died. He wasn't a part of the past that Shane missed. Rob said. "See, it's like you sitting here, right? You've changed, right! Fuck it you even look different, right continental! Fucking lucky I recognized you. That beard geezer, careful it don't go all Noel Edmonds." Shane couldn't help laughing and Lola, who must have started to get the warm fuzzies, kissed them both on the cheek. And maybe Shane was getting a little rush too because he felt that kiss right down to his balls.

After another drink, they got into a taxi and went to a big glass fronted bar with a dance floor up above. They dropped another cheeky half in the taxi over. By the time they arrived everything looked good to Shane. He knew exactly where he was. He knew what he was doing. He knew he was mashed but in a nice way. He had his eyes open but he was going with the flow. He didn't like to admit it but in a way he was happy someone had found him. Happy for the distraction. Anyway as Lola had said, they were just ships passing. He started to drink water.

They danced around to euro crap and cheesy disco with the rest of the punters and made instant dance floor friends with cheeky halves akimbo. They sat at a table off the dance floor that over-looked the street below and smoked a joint one of the dancers had given them. When Lola went to the toilet, Rob got conspiratorial and said to Shane. "Don't take this wrong or nothing but when I first saw you, I thought you'd been sent to -." He trailed off and sat rubbing his nose. Shane said. "Why would Dennis want you dead?" With a shrug, Rob said. "I don't know, because I fucked off I suppose. I don't know and anyway I don't feel like that now. It's great to see you." Shane said. "So, what you were saying earlier, what's it all about, then?" Shifting his shoulders and looking about him, like he thought he was being watched, he said. "I don't know. Maybe Lola's right. I'll just have to get on with it. It's her family and you know what family are like." Sounded like nonsense to Shane, a cover story, so he said. "Okay, right, don't want you giv-ing any family secrets away. I just thought you wanted my help or something."

Rob blew air out of one side of his mouth and his eyes were a bit skew-whiff with the drugs and drink. He said. "I've been with Lola nearly two years now. She's the best thing that ever happened to me. She's opened up my eyes. No offence mate, but she made me see how people used me. I don't want to fuck it up with her, know what I mean?" Shane didn't say anything. He drank some water and looked down at the traffic passing in the street. After a minute or so, Rob said. "Look, don't say anything unless Lola tells you what's what, alright?" Shane nodded. Quietly Rob sighed and said. "It's some sort of fucking hidden treasure or something." Shane half laughed and Rob said. "Don't fucking laugh mate, I think it's true. She's got this photo, right and it's supposed to be where the stuff's hidden. You know that Franco and all that Fascist shit. Well, before that kicked off, her family were bankers. We got to see some old aunt or the other before she pegs it. You know a place called Extremadura?"

Cautious suddenly, Shane said. "Yeh, been there a few times." Rob nodded, pleased and said. "Well that's where it's supposed to be hidden. What's it like?" Shane said. "Countryside mostly." Rob splayed his hands out, palms up on the table. "See, neither Lola nor me have been down there or up there or, fuck it see, I mean I don't even like the countryside, do I? I was thinking maybe you could come along. At least if you were like riding shot-gun, I'd know what was going on. There's money in it, if I can convince Lola to let you come."

Lola came back and when Rob went to the toilet later, Shane looked at Lola and Lola looked at

Shane. Lola had a beautiful smile and her whole face became radiant when she used it. She reached across the table and gently rubbed the top of Shane's arm. She said. "Hey, why so glum? Isn't it lovely to be with friends? Rob may be a little off his tits just now but he's so happy to see you." For a moment Shane didn't think she got it. He didn't give a fuck about Rob and he wasn't glum. He was there because he wanted Lola. She said. "I don't know but it is strange how sometimes with someone there's a connection, like with you. Strange how I saw you first and you saw me. You look better than in the pictures." That took him by surprise but it didn't matter because she smiled again. She said. "Rob's got all this newspaper stuff about you from back when they were looking for you." She stopped. Shane said. "They're still looking."

Somehow her knee rested against his under the table and she managed to look surprised. She said. "Oops." Shane reached beneath the table and touched her knee. Her skin was warm and his fingers tingled. It was her turn to be surprised. She didn't move her leg but licking her lips took a shallow mouthful of air and looking around, said. "No, no *puedo*." She didn't sound completely convinced but Shane put his hands back on the tabletop anyway. Their knees were still touching. He said. "I don't think you saw me first, I think we saw each other at the same time." Lola said. "Rob's a sweetie. I couldn't do this without him, he -." She stopped when she saw Rob coming towards them around the edge of the dance floor and moved her knee. When he sat back down she was all over him and Shane wondered who Rob had ripped off to get this little show on the road. Shane hoped it wasn't Dennis.

In a way, Shane couldn't help himself. Boredom and the little thing between him and Lola made it easy for him to say yes, when, as they parted company in the early hours, Rob had given him a stage wink and said. "I know we're all busy and everything like but what about meeting for breakfast or something?" Lola wasn't short, maybe five seven or eight but Rob was tall. He drew Lola to him and kissed the top of her head. Lola looked straight into Shane's eyes. Rob said. "Well maybe breakfast is fucking pushing it. What about mid-day at that gaff where we met you?"

By eleven thirty, Shane was waiting at the same table drinking a brandy coffee. He felt good with the residue of the E still trolling about in his bloodstream and tweaking his senses. He knew what he was contemplating was a bit stupid but it didn't worry him at that moment. The way he saw it, Lola held the reins and there was nothing he'd ever seen in Rob could change that. Rob had always been someone people used and it takes more than a good B J to cure a personality trait like that. And Lola?

Shane wanted to see what else Lola had to offer. That was what he told himself at least. Really he just wanted to see her and touch her again. If the chance was there he would go along with them to Extremadura, just to feel dry mouthed and awkward around her and to want someone, something, anything, again.

They were late but Shane had been on Spanish time for the last few years so it didn't worry him. Rob looked like he had the night before but more pleased with himself. Lola looked browner in the sunlight, better. She had on a short, close fitting, sleeveless dress with some kind of red and white flowers on it and Doc's. Shane wanted to adjust his vision, move his eyes, look somewhere else but he wanted the kiss when it came. A brush of her lips against his lips. He even let Rob hug him. Fuck it, in for a penny.

Somehow, overnight, Rob had managed to convince Lola that Shane would be an asset. Shane looked at Lola sitting next to Rob. She had a smile on her face that said, if you're coming, it's because I want you to come, everything else is just bullshit. The woman was a piece of work alright, smart and funny, good looking and clever at hiding the fact that she knew it. But she was real too. There was something vibrant with life about her. It didn't matter a fuck to Shane how devious she was. He just wanted to kiss and touch her, to ruffle her up and hear her laugh. He just wanted to fuck her. Rob said. "So, anyway, Lola and I are going fifty-fifty on this. I came up with the stake money and Lola's going to get the family secrets. What I'm fucking saying is, I'll split my take with you. What you reckon?"

Shane didn't need money. The way things were he wouldn't need money for maybe ten years. His isolation cost almost nothing. Spain was still a cheap country. Never-the-less he said. "What's the split?" Scratching his head Rob glanced at Lola but Lola playing her own part, blanked him with a, you're on your own stare. Rob drank his coffee and scratched his head a bit more. "Don't fucking know mate. We don't know what's there. Maybe nothing. Don't even know exactly where it is. It's hard to put a price on it. Fucking hell like, what if I said, twenty-five per cent of my share?" Lola was look- ing at Rob like he was totally bezoomny and for a moment Shane wasn't sure what was going on. Perhaps Rob had changed. Perhaps there was more here than was on show.

Pushing it to see how far it would go, Shane said. "Twenty-five per cent? I want a third of your cut." Lola slapped her thighs with the palms of her hands and pleaded. "Holy mother of the beautiful love! Rob, honey, sweetie, lovely, don't be a *limón*, don't give away everything before you've even got it." Rob looked from one to the other and scratched his head. With a laugh, Shane said. "Look, like Lola said, we're ships in the night. We can all go our own way, nothing's fixed. Rob, you're the first person I know from back then to see me. Last night was a good laugh, thanks." He nodded at Lola. "And you Lola, you've turned this man around. You're a lucky guy, Rob. But I don't want to tag along with you if Lola doesn't want me around. I know how you feel about her and maybe Lola thinks three would be a crowd." Rob said. "Hold on! Fuck sake! She's happy, ain't you lovely?" Stretching out a hand, Rob ran the palm down her arm. "She agreed last night. Told me she just wanted me to be happy." He touched her shoulder and the nape of her neck. "All she's trying to do is protect me." He barked out a laugh. "You want to watch out mate, she's tough." Shane didn't doubt it. Lola was looking at Shane from under her lashes. Shane said. "How much money have you got?" Rob glanced at Lola with shifty eyes. Lola pulled down the corners of her mouth and shifting her gaze to the floor, said. "About 5,000 quid."

It was a double act. Shane knew they were lying and again he wondered what Rob had done. Did the change in Rob's character come from the fact that he couldn't go back? Lola said. "Hey chaps, let's not make this all about money. Last night we were friends. All this thirds stuff is like a fly in the jam. Can't we just wait and see -." She left it hanging and glanced from Rob to Shane. Shane looked at the shape of her face and the darkness of her brown eyes and the red in her hair with the sun on it. Everything was a balance and Shane had been balanced for a long time. Fuck that! He'd come to Madrid for some fun and excitement. Maybe this was really it.

3

They plodded slowly up a red dirt path between tall trees. It was the dog days of early August and Extremadura was mid-summer dry. Nobody spoke. The heavy packs and the stifling heat took care of that and Shane was glad. Rob was in the lead. Lola was next. Shane last. He didn't completely trust Lola, nor did he completely trust the new Rob and he didn't even trust himself around Lola. A clutch of small, colourful, birds came out of a bush and flew across the path in front of Rob. He went. "Fuck me! Did you see that! "

Neither Lola nor Shane answered. Looking over his shoulder, Rob said. "Oi, Lola lovely, what's the name of those birds?" Lola didn't answer and Rob repeated the question. After a brief silence and a sigh, Lola said, wearily. "How would I know darling, I'm from Madrid. Like London, we got pigeons." Rob carried on walking. After a few paces, he tried again. "Come on Shane man, you must know. You speak fucking pukka Spanish and like you been living here like for a few years." Shane watched Lola walking along before him and said, evenly. "Fuck the birds. Where's this house?" Not stopping, Rob turned around to face them and walking backwards, said. "I know what you mean, mate. This fucking rucksack's killing me. I told you we should have driven up." Rob turned around again. They walked on. Shane knew the birds were Bee Eaters. Almost despite himself, he reached out and touched her bare arm. Lola turned her head and looked at Shane, then looked back up the track.

A boulder the size of a house covered in dried-out moss and with a couple of twisted, dwarf oaks sprouting out of the top, sent the path off at a sharp right angle. Once around the corner the trail widened and rose steeply to a kind of *mesa*. Rob half staggered, half ran the last twenty yards and throwing his rucksack on the ground, spread his arms wide and said excitedly. "At last! This is it! Got to be, ain't it! What do you reckon, Lola lovely?" From the look of Lola she didn't reckon much at all at that time. It had been a stiff walk and not the first one they had made that day in their search. She was blowing hard and when she reached Rob, just walked around him, dropped her baggage and flopped to the ground. In his joy, Rob didn't seem to notice. Instead he trotted forward to meet Shane and take his rucksack. Shane stopped and let him lift it from his shoulders. What was the point of doing anything else? He didn't like the way the man kowtowed to him but Rob talked a lot and anything that stopped him, even for a second, was good with Shane.

Lola was drinking water out of a bottle and Shane went over to her while Rob carried over his stuff. Squatting down in front of her, he said, in Spanish. "Can I have a drink?" She had the bottle close up to her mouth. She licked her lips and winked at him. Shane held out his hand. Lola turned her head away from him and while smiling up at Rob and passing the bottle to Shane, replied in Spanish. "Anything you want." Rob said. "What she say?" Shane told Rob again, he thought it would be a good idea if he learned a little Spanish. But Rob was in a kind of evangelical frame of mind, he said. "Fuck that, come on let's look around. This has got to be it."

While Shane drank water and Lola lolled, he went almost dancing from corner to corner of the plateau, like an excited kid. "Look at it. Don't tell me this is natural. It's just like too flat and it's not like we're near the top of anything or anything. Come on you two, look. There's fucking trees everywhere but here. It's obvious. It's like when they find Eldorado in some film or something or some fucking famous mummy's tomb or something, fuck man everybody knows, it's like the fucking place, you know? Check it out. I bet if I scrabble about a bit there'll be bricks and bits of metal and shit like they dig up in those fucking T V programmes about Vikings and shit. Look at it, it's got to be the place!"

Shane sat down and rested back on the pile of baggage. He wasn't quite sure if he wanted to find anything. He told himself what he wanted was Lola. Sure he wanted some of the treasure if it was here but he didn't want trouble, didn't want to get noticed and why would he? For the past four years he'd lived trouble free less, than fifty K's away. When they set out he didn't realize how exposed he would feel travelling with other people, especially when one of those people was Rob. Shane's bit of comfort came from the fact that if push came to shove, he could do a Laurie Lee on it and almost hike home through the mountains. His house and how he lived was something this pair knew nothing about. They believed, like most ex-pats, he lived down on the Brit coast.

Shane looked around. Rob was right. The *mesa* was unnaturally flat for such a large open space, with the rest of the mountain rearing up behind like a wedge had been cut out of it. There were plenty of trees and scrub growing across the open space but nothing like the mature forest that surrounded it. Rob was on his knees under a bush. Lola took out the wallet that held her passport and other documents from the pocket of her shorts and removed the photograph. It was a small black and white picture of a large hunting lodge. Shane had seen it plenty of times before. The photo was old and grainy but the lodge still looked pretty impressive. Stone and timber built with a wide covered terrace on three sides. There were people on the terrace and cars parked outside.

The first time he'd seen it, Shane guessed it at sometime in the nineteen-twenties. Lola swore it was early nineteen-thirty. It was, Lola insisted, significant. If what the old lady had said was true, then Lola was right, it was significant. It was why they were here. If Rob had the idea that between him and Shane there was some kind of an old times sake thing, like they were mates, then he was as much of a fool as he'd ever been. Only chance had brought them together again. True, Shane had earned a lot of money out of Rob when the bean thing really took off but that was it and that was then. This wasn't about friendship, mate-ship or any other kind of shit. Everything about what they were doing here was about self-interest, pure self-interest, even Shane's desire.

Getting to her feet, Lola looked at the photo and shading her eyes, scanned the *mesa* . She walked some steps, looked about, turned and walked the other way. She tilted her head and tried another angle. Catching Shane's eye, she pulled her mouth down and her eyes wide and shrugged her shoulders as if to say, who knows? This wasn't the first track they had tried that day and they were all tired. Standing up, Shane went over to her and studied the snap over her shoulder, just to be close to her. "Look at this!" Rob pulled himself out of the bushes, "I told you! Look, look!" He held up a piece of glass. It was maybe 150mm long, seventy or so wide and about 5mm thick. Lola put the picture in the back pocket of her jeans and took the piece of glass, she said. "This ain't Mars Rob, honey, people been here before." Shane liked the way Lola spoke English, the languid way she used all the little bits of slang and cleverness, like she'd been speaking it all her life. Before Rob could answer, she waved an arm behind her to the way they had come. "Didn't you see the path, sweetie? People come hiking here all the time." Rob took back the piece of glass and passed it to Shane. What the fuck did Shane know about glass? Nothing. He took it and looked at it. To him it looked like a piece of window glass. He handed it back to Rob and shrugged. Rob wanted more, he said. "Come on! No I mean it. We're all in this now. Fucking hell!" He kicked out and a stone scuttled off into the bushes. Touching his arm, Lola said gently. "Hey don't be a grouch, lovely. Look, let's look at the snappy snap and see if we can see anything."

She took the photograph out of her pocket and Rob took it out of her hand, he said. "What? So it doesn't matter what I think, right? What I feel? But if you think you can see something in this fucking picture, which even your old aunt said, may mean nothing, then this is the place, right? Fuck that." He flipped the photo back to her and Lola caught it. To Shane, he said. "See all those trees and the bushes over there? See how they run in lines?" He cut straight lines in the air with his arms and said. "Foundations, cellars, shit like that. Saw a thing about it on the telly. That's how they find those old Stone Age forts and that. Aerial photographs." He stamped a foot on the ground a couple of times. "This was probably where those cars were parked." They stood around and checked the photo as best they could against the bit of land and if you had a good imagination or wanted what was supposed to be there bad enough, then, it was the place. And it was the place because Rob jabbed a finger at the photo. "Fuck me, am I the only one here with fucking eyes? Look, that thing that looks like a shadow, ain't that that fucking boulder? Am I right or am I fucking right?" They all looked again. Shane didn't like to admit it, but Rob was right. Lola circled her arms around his waist, rested her head against his chest and stared up at him like he was God. She said. "You're the bees knees, lovely. I just love a *hombre* who brings home the *jamón*." Rob glowed and grinned. Even he knew the meaning of *hombre* and *jamón*. They pitched camp.

Shane put his tent a bit away from Rob and Lola's spot. They had been travelling together for several days. For some reason Lola had wanted to go the long way around. Roaming here and there in the 4x4 with them for hours on end was hard enough. Then eating together and staying at the same hotel at night and often as not having a room next to theirs wasn't perfect. He'd spent less time alone with Lola than in Madrid. Now he didn't need to hear any more of their intimate moments. But it was more than that. Over the days they'd been together Shane had realized he had a problem with Rob that really had nothing to do with him wanting Lola.

The man was a part of another life and Shane couldn't help but see him as he was at their first encounter. It was down on one of those container parks in some manky bit of Kent before the Chunnel. Rob was like a debt payment. People owed Shane money and Rob owed them money. It was a working relationship that Rob could never get out from under. Three days before he had been shut in an empty container, by the people he owed the money to. They had taken all his clothes and locked him up in the complete dark. Shane became his new master. He still owed as much money as he had before but by the time Shane came to collect him he was grateful to be alive. When Shane had thrown back the doors, Rob had rushed out of the container like a mad man. Naked and slicked in shit, he had tried to hug Shane's knees. Shane had jumped back and kicked him out of the way. There was nothing left in the man, he just fell down crying and said. "Yeh, whatever you say."

Rob was a dealer. He wasn't a businessman and he wasn't a criminal and that was his problem. But thousands of pounds passed through Rob's hands every week. Sometimes, every day. To the criminals that supplied him, he was a kind of milk cow, a muppet on a string and that was what he'd been to Shane as well. What he couldn't figure now was how Rob had gotten free from that grindstone. When Shane had bargained him on he still owed close on forty grand. No matter what he did, the people who owned him would have made sure he didn't have that kind of money, ever, the same way Shane had.

Across the space separating them, Shane could hear Rob talking to Lola. Telling her to put this here and that there and how he knew he'd been right and how they should have just driven the fucking vehicle straight up, 'cause what was the point of hiring a 4 x 4 if you only fucking drove it on the road and anyway now they needed water to make tea and shit like that and how he wasn't walking back all that way 'cause someone had to stay here and he wanted to check the place out to see if he could find anything before it got dark. Lola said. "Okey dokey lovely, whatever you say Rob. I like a stroll darling." Shane couldn't figure it, couldn't work out the power between them. The way Lola went along massaging Rob's ego or even how Rob had managed to get a woman like Lola in the first place. What he had realized over their time together was that they were a kind of a team.

By the time the tents were erected it was early evening and the desperate heat of the day was beginning to wane. Shane lay on his sleeping bag on the floor of the tent, hands behind his head, thinking how good a siesta would be. With a cough, Rob knocked on the open tent flap like it was a door. After a few seconds, when Shane didn't respond, Rob stuck his head inside. The weak, slippery grin of the messenger with a favour to ask was slapped across his face and it was an attitude Shane recognized far easier than the man with a plan that Rob was trying to project.

He said. "All right Shane, mate? Lola was thinking of going down and bringing the motor up and I was wondering like, if you'd take a wander down there with her?" With a sigh Shane sat up, came out of the tent and said, jokingly. "What's up with you, got broken legs or something?" Rob giggled and felt his legs, he said. "Fuck me! That's what's wrong! I wondered why I couldn't walk! Thanks man! I could have gone forever and never noticed." His shoulders were hunched and when he laughed at his own joke, he pulled his neck further down into shoulders and nodded his head like some old turkey. Shane sighed. Rob still grinning his slidey grin, tried to sound sympathetic, he said. "Yeh I know. I told Lola when we were down on the road she should have driven straight up."

His nose was big and pockmarked and the colour of dirty putty. He giggled, rubbed a hand under it like it was running and said. "Who'd have thought, eh? You and me up a mountain like this! Life's weird. But lucky man! I was feeling -." For a moment his face drooped a bit and his fingers fluttered and then it was all blue skies again and he said. "Yeh, yeh, well I was feeling a bit isolated like. Not speaking da' lingo and that and Lola doing everything. You know, her rabbitting on and people looking at me like I'm stupid or something." Shane said. "Yeh?" Rob had stopped smiling. He said. "Yeh. Anyway, fuck it, come on."

Neither Shane nor Lola spoke as they walked back down the track. Nor did they touch. Long shadows were dropping over the path in chunks, chopped up by blinding swathes of late sun. Insects filled the blocks of sunlight and they could smell pine and wild rosemary. Both were careful. A sense of what they wanted was strong in them both.

Their reasons for not taking it were different.

Although in his thirties, Shane had never been in love and he wasn't in love with Lola. He was a tad infatuated, sure. He wanted her body, her smiles and her touch. He didn't need to know her star sign but he'd listen if she wanted to tell him. He'd been around her long enough now, not to believe half of what she said but that didn't matter, like her star sign didn't matter. Years of crime had attuned Shane's senses and he did almost believe in the hidden treasure, especially now they had found the ruins of the house. But there was something else as well. To Shane it didn't matter what Rob and Lola said or did and it didn't matter if he and Lola did anything, what mattered was adrenalin, that buzz of excitement he didn't even know he'd missed until they had come along. Now even just walking down the track with nothing happening, he could taste it in the back of his throat.

On the other hand, Lola had been an only child and although her parents had died when she was a teenager, she had been a spoilt child and didn't even know it. She was selfish in everything as though it was her right. She had worked hard when she first arrived in London because she didn't have a choice but had never considered it her natural role to serve the aged or anyone. To Lola work in any real sense was for other people and since she'd hooked up with Rob, she expected to be looked after. Before she met Rob, she was often a yellow jacket in the fluffy club scene. These were the kind of clubs where Rob did some of his business. What Lola did was be all smiley like and offer free hugs and stamp peoples wrists on the door with a fluorescent stamp. It was a social scene and once you'd done a couple of hours, you got in for free. That was how she and Rob had first come to meet. At a chill out party, just being part of the scene, you know. Now when she yellow jacketed she was more of a conduit for Rob than anything but that was okay because E's sold with almost no effort. It was easy money. She didn't have to change old people's nappies anymore.

Lola had heard stories about Shane from Rob long before their meeting in Madrid. He was almost a hero to Rob. She couldn't understand why he had been so proud to know this thug, this killer. It just didn't go with the whole fluffy scene they were involved in, even if Rob was a dealer. Now she didn't know. Desperation changes everything. It had changed her. She didn't know what people were capable of anymore or even what she was capable of. That was the trouble with the world, everyone seemed normal but nobody was. Okay they had pulled a stroke in London to set themselves up but it had amazed her when Rob had first seen Shane and he'd wanted to run away, believing he'd been sent to kill him. It didn't change her view of Shane but it had changed her view of Rob. In London Rob had seemed very capable and a free spirit, with money. A bit dodgy yes and so different from a lot of the mummies boys she'd met in England. But once they were in Spain he had become like a little kid and she had to do everything from ordering food, to buying his new razors. Lola had been looking after herself since she was seventeen and she wasn't into looking after other people.

Lola wanted. She couldn't help herself, she'd always wanted, even before the death of her family. It didn't matter what it was, she wanted whatever it was she thought had been kept from her. In Madrid her own desperation had surprised even her. She had stepped over a line. There was nowhere to go back to and nobody to save her. It didn't matter. What was done was done and now it was shit or bust. From Lola's way of looking at the world, anything they found here was hers by right. She would agree to share but that did not mean she would share. Although Rob was a sweetie, she didn't feel she owed him anything. Maybe like he said, he really loved her but it didn't matter to Lola. Ultimately he was someone she could manipulate and leave in her wake. She wasn't so sure about Shane and watched him from the corner of her eye as they walked side by side.

4

The *Guardia Civil's* car was parked up next to the 4x4 and the cops inside got out when they saw them approaching. Shane had been avoiding the cops ever since he was a teen and to him the *Gaurdia Civil* didn't seem quite as thick or as vindictive as the average Brit cop but that didn't mean they weren't cops. Then again, the cops weren't looking for him here. In Spain he was a good citizen.

Way back in Franco's time they had sported those weird tri-cornered hats. Back then people said that if you joined the *Guardia*, you declared civil war on the people. Nowadays they were friendlier and in some of those half dead towns that litter Spain, it was often the only decent job around. Once he'd been stopped late at night coming out of some nondescript town outside of Barcelona. He'd had a drink but he wasn't drunk. The *Guardia* had breathalysed him and he was over the limit. The pair of cops pulled faces and had a little confab. In the end one had asked him what football team he supported. Shane didn't know shit about football but he should have known Real Madrid was the wrong answer. They laughed like it was all a joke but put him in the cells for six hours before deciding he was sober enough to go. When he'd told Jesus, he had laughed his head off and said. "Ah my friend, the football question is always the hardest question to answer." There were also dozens of arbitrary on the spot fines they could drop on you if you were rude or arrogant. Shane favoured smiles and politeness and the idea that he really only spoke English. After all, these guys carried side arms and sometimes machine guns.

One was fiftyish with a brandy red nose, and a flabby body straining to escape the tight green uniform. The other was all *Nuevo España*, tall and young and good looking, if you liked men in uniform. He hung back almost shyly, while the older guy did the talking. "*Buenas tardes, Senores.*" Like the young cop, Shane wanted to stay in the background and stepped away from Lola. She glanced at him and he was surprised to see an edge of fear in her eyes. Maybe she thought he would do the man thing and take over. Instead he gave her a stupid British look and smiled. Lola swallowed and said.

"*Buenas tardes.*" The cop looked from one to the other. With a smidge of distain in his eyes for Shane and his idiot smile, he said, to Lola. "*Es este coche suya, señorita?* (Is the car yours, miss?)" For the first time since he'd met her Lola seemed on the back foot. She fumbled around in the patch pockets of her shorts, pulling out the wallet containing her passport, driving licence, vehicle rental papers and then dropping this and that and apologizing and smiling at the fat cop and picking stuff up and dropping something else, as she nervously answered. "*No, no es un coche alquilado.* (No the car is rented.)" Shane didn't try to help or make things better. He kept his stupid smile on and listened.

As he went through the papers, the *Guardia* asked the stock questions. Where have you come from? Where are you going? You live in London, yes? Although the answers didn't seem to interest him, he watched Lola closely as she stumbled over her replies. Somehow the photo of the old lodge had got in amongst the rental papers. Glancing at it casually, he held it out to Lola but before she could take it back, looked again. He peered at it. Turned it to the light to get a better view, tapped it on his thumbnail thoughtfully and turned the snap over to see if anything was written on the back. Lola's hand was still out and Shane could see her fingers trembling a little, as though she wanted to grab the photo back. When he passed it to her, she took it quickly and put it away in a pocket. Turning now with fresh interest to Shane, the cop held out his hand.

His meaning was obvious but Shane shrugged, pulled a don't understand face and smiled inanely. Maybe these two had run into a few thick Brits because almost in unison, they said. *"Pasaporte!"* The younger *Guardia* straightened up to his full height as he spoke, rested a hand on the butt of his pistol and eyeballed Shane. Shane smiled full into his eyes and passed his passport to the chubby one. They took all the papers and went over to their car. The older one opened the driver's side door and sat half in, half out. The young one squatted beside him. They perused the passports and hire contract, looking up every few seconds as though something was about to occur. Lola tried to speak to Shane but he blanked her and turned his head away. Silence was almost always best.

After a few minutes they came over and gave back the papers. Everything seemed to be in order, but Shane could almost smell their suspicion on the rise, especially the older one. Fuck them, was Shane's attitude but for once he was not the focus of police attention. No, for some reason they were more interested in Lola and began to question her again. What was the purpose of her visit? How long did they intend to stay in the area? Where were they staying? Did they have a hotel booked? Did she understand camping was forbidden in the forest? Was she aware of the danger of forest fires? Where did she intend to go next? Did she still have family in Madrid? Blah, blah, blah. Lola was like someone trapped in a corner and having tennis balls fired at her. For a moment Shane thought she was acting. She ducked and dived and fielded the questions as best she could with vague and incomplete answers. But she physically winced when a ball hit home and was almost in tears when she told them that both her parents were dead. The young *Guardia* looked shamefaced for a moment but the older one smiled.

Shane stepped in then, closing the gap between himself and Lola with a gob full of fast English he knew they wouldn't understand. "Hold up, hold on, what's this all about! What's she done? What have we done! We stop and go for a bit of an old leg stretch and you lot are all over us. Everything's in order, ain't it? What you upsetting her for? Look at her. She's almost in tears. Come here darling, come on here." Shane pulled Lola to him like they were lovers, put his arm around her shoulders and stared at the cops. It stopped their questions but the older one had a nasty twist to his mouth, like he wanted to batter somebody. The younger just looked embarrassed. They exchanged cop type looks. The arrogant lift of the chin, coupled with that unsure little sideways pull of the mouth.

Relieved, Lola snuggled into Shane and gave him a sweetie, lovely, honey overdose he didn't need. Then the older *Guardia*, thinking Shane couldn't understand Spanish, addressed Lola. There was a sneering, mock disbelief in his voice as he said. "Ha, so this is what the high and mighty Varela's have come to, is it? Is this why good Spanish girls go to London? Mmm, to fuck red neck English, hooligans? Take him away from us before we show him some real Spanish hospitality." He paused for effect and then went on. "We, him and me." He jerked a thumb at his partner. "We'll be watching you, *señorita* Varela. Some names never die in the memory of the people." Shane didn't know what he was on about and he looked at chubby's partner and by the look on the young guy's face, he didn't know what the fuck was going on either. Then to Shane's amazement, Lola said, harshly. "*¿ Qué significa un nombre? ¿ Ninguno de su familia hacer nal?* (What does a name mean? Did none of your family ever do wrong?)" Chubby didn't like it. He stared at Lola in silence, his top lip pulled back like a dog ready to bite. The young *Guardia* peered uneasily at his partner and at Lola and Shane. It was the moment when things could have turned nasty for everybody. The wrong thing done or said and things could simply go pear.

Shane had already decided he wasn't going anywhere with these guys anyway. Holding Lola and feeling her arm snaked around his waist, he just wanted to disappear with her for a few hours. The two *Guardia Civil* didn't mean shit to him. Before chubby could do anything to make matters worse, the young one decided to take charge. Reaching out, he took the passports and the hire papers out of his partner's hand and said. "Here are your papers, you can go. There is nothing more." They got into the 4x4, Lola at the wheel. She was holding it together, just. Shane said. "Do you want me to drive?" She shook her head. By the time the engine was started the young one was back at the side window. Lola's shoulders drooped but she slid the window down and maybe that was something else Shane liked about her, the combination of strength and vulnerability. The cop said. "*Sólo por nuestros, ¿a donde se va ahora?* (Just for our records, where are you going now?)" Her face went all pinched up and she closed her eyes and as she spoke, she hit the steering wheel with her fist. "*Vamos en ses pueblo de nuevo allí para tomar una copa! ¿Está bien?* (We are going into that town back there to have a drink! Is that okay!)" She didn't wait for an answer but raised the window, jammed the car into gear and pulled away. Lola said. "*Putas!!*" Half a minute later the *Guardia Civil* followed.

Shane watched Lola. Her chin and mouth were fixed for survival. Her nostrils moved slightly as she took fast, short breaths like someone fighting back tears. Shane wanted to touch her again but she was locked into a frequency of her own. Her eyes didn't look anywhere but the road or the rear view mirror, where the cops were. They drove on, tipping the speed limit, in silence. The patrol car followed them until they reached the half-arsed town and stopped outside a bar. They sat in the 4x4 while it slowly passed them and accelerated down the street. Lola was shaking.

When the cop car was gone, she dropped her head onto the steering wheel and said, quietly. "Fuck a duck." Shane took the opportunity to put an arm around her shoulder again. Although he didn't altogether believe what he was saying, he said. "Come on, it's alright. They got no real interest in us. Anyway, we ain't done anything, we're just holidaymakers. They're just being cops." She looked up at him from the steering wheel, then lifted her head and moved her hand from the gear stick to his thigh. She said. "I'm not a one horse pony, you know." Shane let her fingers creep up under the edge of his shorts before putting his hand over hers. As he came in to kiss her, he said, mockingly. "No, no *puedo*." Lola gave a throaty little laugh and then they fell on each other. Kissing her, the way her body felt as he ran his hands over it, the warmth and texture of her skin, her lips, her tongue around his, all of it was what he wanted. He shifted the idea of money and consequences to another part of his mind. Fuck it. At that moment pleasure was having his hand down Lola's shorts.

In a moment when they weren't kissing or looking into each other's eyes, they saw the *Guardia's* car coming back up the street towards them. As it reached their vehicle, it slowed and crawled past. The two cops stared in at them. Lola froze and for a moment, Shane saw real fear in her eyes. Her nails dug into his thigh, her voice trembled as she said. "What shall we do?" Shane took his arm from her shoulders and gently disengaged her hand from his thigh, he said. "Come on, let's go in the bar for a drink. Fuck them, they'll soon get bored."

For a moment then, she was troubled by another thought, she said. "What about Rob? He'll go bonkers." Shane didn't give a fuck about Rob and it still surprised him that she did, he said. "Why?" Maybe his lack of interest showed in his voice because Lola looked nonplussed and as though nothing had happened between Shane and herself, said. "The sweetie doesn't like being left alone, especially here in Spain. Once in London I stayed out clubbing all night without him and he went mad and was gloomy for weeks, the darling!" Shane shook his head and sighed. He wasn't the jealous type but he really didn't want to know. What he wanted was Lola and she knew it. Tilting her head and taking his head in her hands, she kissed him on the mouth. She said. "Sometimes men are just too silly!" She kissed him again and said softly. "Don't you like to be wanted? I like to be wanted and Rob loves me. Don't be a grouch, please and let us not judge each other."

Inside they sat at the bar. The other patrons sat together at tables watching one of those never-ending Spanish quiz shows. The owner, who was sitting at a table with his customers, disengaged himself from the telly just long enough to serve them. They sat and faced each other on bar stools. Shane said. "What's with the *Guardia*? Is there something I should know?" Lola wouldn't look at him directly and Shane kissed her and made her look into his eyes. Quietly he said. "I ain't no sweetie, honey, darling, so don't bother with that. Why are you worried about the cops, eh?" Lola smooched up to him and stroked his face and placed a hand on his thigh again. Shane knew he was being smoozed but didn't care. She said. "I was worried about you. You told me they were still after you." Shane wasn't convinced and took the passport out of his pocket and showed her. It was in the name of someone called Brian Johnston. He said. "Don't worry about me, they ain't after me. Look Lola, what did you and Rob do before you left London? Who did you rip off? Is someone looking for you? Not the cops, no?"

Lola looked at him with her big eyes and in those eyes Shane saw that he'd hit home somewhere and kissed her. It didn't matter what she said and it didn't matter what lies she told. There was something more than treasure involved. She said. "Maybe Rob owes some money, you know, to people. That's why he thought you'd been sent to kill him." She waved a hand. "But that's just a fly in the jam. Who would ever look for us here?" Shane couldn't help but admire the way she could look him in the eye and lie. Something definitely wasn't right. There was more to it than either Rob or Lola was letting on to. Nobody who had the use of Rob would kill him over the money he owed. What use was he dead? The most he could have ripped off from Dennis was his own weekly take. You didn't kill the laying hen. He was just on a long chain that was all. Sooner or later he would go back again, what else could he do? Shane didn't bother to push it or explain his take on things, instead he said. "Let's have another drink and get back to Rob before he gets too spooked up there on his own. This is probably the nearest he's ever been to the great outdoors."

As they drove out of town, Shane watched for the police but there was no sign of them. It was dark as they crawled up the track, low branches and bushes brushing against the 4x4 as Lola struggled with the gears and cursed like a fishwife. Shane laughed, he said. "Where on earth did you learn your English?" She stopped the vehicle. The lights on full beam made a tripped out cavern of the track and the trees ahead. Every kind of winged bug was throwing itself into the light, on a crazy death mission. A nervous sweat, beaded her forehead. She said. "In London I drive a Punto. This thing scares the holy shit out of me." Shane put his hand on hers on the wheel. She said. "It's alright. The police upset me, I don't know why. And my English, blimey chap, what is wrong with my English init? Well, mostly I learned to swear from the old men at the old peoples home. They are like Rob, fuck this, fuck that, every other word. The old ladies are always love, darling, ducks and saying things like, all mouth and trousers and by hook or by crook and all sorts of things that don't make sense. I think sometimes I misheard what they said. I know what I say is wrong sometimes but I like sound of the words -." She kissed him and said. "Don't say anything to Rob, please." Shane said. "You mean about you being a one horse pony?" She smiled and said. "Yes." He said. "As long as I'm not a fly in the jam." She laughed and playfully punched his arm, before putting the car in gear.

To Lola most men were stupid but you had to watch out for their egos. Some could even surprise you. Rob had. It didn't stop him being stupid but really he was kind and gentle and generous, she could see that. It didn't mean much to her. She would she thought, be sad when they parted company. With only Rob to deal with everything had seemed so much simpler. Sooner or later she planned to loose Rob but keep the London money and if there was anything here, all of that as well. Was there anything? Somehow after years of dreaming it was now almost too real for Lola. She believed they were in the right place. Something had to be here. All she had to do was find the spot. Or let Rob find the spot. It didn't matter anymore if there was a fortune or just some old bits of jewellery. But whatever it was she wanted it.

Since her parent's death, locating this supposed lost fortune had been the driving force in her life. To get something back from a world that had taken everything from her. Rob said they didn't need it anymore but he didn't understand that it was more than just money. As far as Shane went she found him as attractive as she ever found anyone. She knew what most men wanted when they saw her and he wasn't any different. At least he was cute. She would wait and see what occurred. What surprised her about men was what most men wanted she didn't often have to give. She had hands. She had tricks. She had a mouth. Men were easily satisfied. Some men she wanted to fuck so she fucked them. Some men she didn't and sometimes she fucked them. With Shane she hadn't decided yet.

Mostly she didn't want him to get nasty. The newspaper articles Rob had kept, made him sound like an animal. Now she didn't know and she didn't want to think about what she was or what she had done.

The huge rock with the tree on top leered over them in the headlights. Lola almost stalled the engine as she tried to drop a gear, in the tight right turn but cursing, she gunned the engine and they shot up the last steep incline onto the *mesa*. The headlights swept over Rob as he stood, a lonely hunched figure in a sleeveless puffa jacket, one hand in his pocket and the other shading his eyes. He was at Lola's door before the engine had stopped turning. His face had the look of someone who'd been stuck at the bottom of a well for a week. He said. "Fucking hell, fuck me, you're back! Thank fuck for that! Fuck sake, you been gone for ever and a fucking day. Three fucking hours! Believe me that is like forever up here on your lonesome." Lola got out and wrapped him in her arms and kissed him quiet with a dozen darlings, sweeties and honeys. She explained about the *Guardia* and how they had gone to a bar in the nearest town, to get rid of them. Unlike Lola, Rob didn't seem bothered by the police but was more interested in whether they had brought back any beers. They hadn't. Shane watched Rob closely. Maybe he wasn't the jealous type, maybe he really trusted Lola or maybe he understood things better than Shane gave him credit for.

As well as two gas Tilly lamps, Rob had a little fire going near his tent and everything looked cosy with the red glow and the white-yellow flames licking the dark and sparks rising in the grey smoke to the sky. Shane got one of the spades from the back of the 4x4 and shovelled earth over it until it was out. Rob moaned good humouredly with a pile of fuck this, fuck that's and what the fucks. Shane said. "Fuck this, fuck that, fuck whatever but we're all fucked if this lot goes up." He waved an arm at the tinder dry forest that surrounded them. The city boy in Rob didn't give a toss about the fire or the forest. After three hours on his old oddy knoky, he would have felt justified if he'd burned the lot down.

Happy to be with other humans again, Rob just wanted to talk. Throwing up his arms, he grinned and said. "Man! You take away a man's little bit of comfort and don't even bring him a beer! I thought we were camping, you know? Ging gang goolie all round the campfire, poor little lambs that have gone astray and all that shit." He laughed and hooked an arm around Lola's shoulders. "It's so good to have you back, lovely." He raised a thumb at Shane. "Glad she was with you, mate. Yeh, sorry about the fire, I forgot or like I didn't forget, know what I mean? I just got lonely out here in the dark." Rob hadn't forgotten, he'd simply wanted a fire. A little fire, what the fuck harm could there be in that? Rob never expected anything to go wrong although things went wrong in his life all the time.

Mostly the things that went wrong were normal shit he simply brushed off, other stuff he endured. Rob had been dealing since he was thirteen or fourteen. Only son of a junkie mum off a Deptford estate, he'd learnt early it didn't matter what he did as long as he survived. Selling drugs was a lifestyle and a career, like an access all areas pass. Plenty of people were pleased to see him. Sometimes the shit hit the fan and he got robbed, ripped off or nicked. There was nothing to do then but shrug and take it. For years he had owed more money than he could ever hope to come up with but yet he always had money. The people that supplied him thought he didn't understand what they did to him but he did. He just didn't care.

He went through life and he tried to make the best of it. Until Lola came along, Rob thought the world was fucked. The world was still fucked but now he had Lola and that had changed everything. To him Lola was the only thing of worth in his life. He didn't understand how it had happened, didn't even try to understand. All he knew was that every time she wasn't with him it was like he was holding his breath until she got back. As far as he could see, they were in it together. The soft part of Rob that had never been battered out of him, believed they would find the treasure and maybe even live happily ever after. As far as Shane went, although Rob had been frightened out of his socks on first seeing him, now his company gave him confidence. A third of his share didn't bother him that much. They already had money and it was good to have a man like Shane in your corner just in case.

Shane went to his tent and came back with the bottle of J&B he had in his pack and gave it to Rob. He didn't exactly know why. It was almost like he felt sorry for the man and that kind of irritated him. Rob was over the moon. He did a little dance, drunk a swift couple of caps full and made a speech about people and forward planning, toasting Shane. Shane said. "This is mostly national park now and this definitely ain't a fucking designated campsite. If the cops come back again or if we have a fire or even if some nosey hikers report us for camping, we'll be chucked off here. Let's just try to cast a low profile, eh?"

They sat on chunks of rock around the dead campfire and ate bread and ham with ripe plum tomatoes and little dill pickles out of the jar. Out of the blue, Rob said. "How old are you, Shane?" The J&B was in Shane's hand. He looked down at the bottle. Rob said, laughingly. "Alright, nothing funny, just wondering that's all." Shane took a gulp and passed the bottle to Lola. He said. "Why?" Rob sighed. "I've thought about a lot of shit while I've been with Lola. Look, me I'm thirty eight." He flourished a hand as if to say, there that didn't hurt. Shane laughed and said. "No really? You look much older! Don't you think he looks older Lola?" Lola gave the bottle to Rob and in a low, throaty voice, said. "No, no in the morning he is so choochie. You know like a little rosy cheeked school boy, the real bee's knees. Come on Shane don't be a grouch, what age are you?" Taking the whisky bottle, Shane took a gulp and said. "Thirtyish." Rob said. "See?" Shane said. "What?" Rob said. "You know, for some reason, all the time I worked for you I thought you were older than me. Everybody seems older than me, always have done. Fucking weird that. Lola reckons it's because I expect people to take advantage of me." Shane said. "Business is business. I didn't get you in debt. And I don't give a fuck what age you are." Lola gave a cynical laugh. Passing the bottle, Shane held up his hands and said to Rob. "I didn't treat you no worse than anybody else, did I?" Rob looked at Lola and she reached a hand out and rubbed his knee. Rob said. "It don't matter now, water under the bridge and all that. Things ain't the same anymore. I'm out of all that." Shane said. "Still owe Dennis money?" Rob didn't look at Shane but said emphatically. "No man, fucking no. All the years I've been at it I shouldn't owe no-cunt nothing." That wasn't what Shane had asked but he kept quiet.

The bottle was in Lola's hand. She raised it above her head and said. "Come on chaps no need to get all gloomy about the past." Maybe she was a little bit tipsy but Shane didn't think so. She drank and passed the bottle on. She giggled. She said. "Everything is okey dokey." Rob was grinning foolishly at her, happy because she was happy and that made him happy. Shane felt like puking. Rob said. "Too right my lovely. The past's another country and all that fucking shit. Fuck it, this is another country and we've all got fucking past's ain't we?" Passing the bottle to Shane, he said. "See, way I see it you got away clean. Whoosh! It was like you didn't exist anymore. And if we hadn't run into you, you still wouldn't exist. Well, you would wouldn't you like, somewhere but not here, yeh? Anyway, all I'm saying is you got away and that's all we want to do. Leave all that shit behind us."

Shane didn't bother to tell Rob that part of the cost of getting away, had been giving him to Dennis. Instead he stood up and taking a last pull on the J&B, handed the bottle back to Lola and said. "Why should you have any problems? You ain't running away from anything, right? Anyway, I'm knackered, I'm going to bed." Lola jumped up, hugged him and kissed his cheek. Shane put his hands in his pockets to stop himself touching her. She said. "Thanks for helping with the policeman."

Rob raised a thumb and said. "Yeh. And tomorrow we treasure hunt! I got a good feeling about this." In his tent Shane lay and listened to the rustle of little critters in the undergrowth and the creaking, whispering forest all around. He could hear the murmur of Rob and Lola's voices as they sat out in the ambient night polishing off the rest of the drink. Later he heard them shooshing each other as they stumbled around. He heard the 4x4's door open. There was murmuring and a shoosh here and a shoosh there and the closing click of the car door. Then he heard them stumble back to their tent.

5

They had *huevos* and fried tomatoes, sopped up with the rest of the bread for breakfast. Rob was all get up and go, dragging out the spades and the metal detectors from the motor. Shane grinned, he said. "Very professional!" Rob wagged one of the metal detectors and said. "Don't fucking laugh mate, sophisticated little fuckers these! Sorts it all out, screens for dross. You want gold, that's what it buzzes for. Silver? The same. This is like state of the fucking art. Better than digital it's practically computerized mate, it's got fucking ram, bits and bites, anti-roll bars and satellite navigation. Like, this baby's got automatic read out and a talking fucking clock, it's got anti theft alarms, it's got solar panels, it's environmentally fucking mental and it's got go faster stripes and is totally GPS enabled. Hoist a sail and you could go all around the world in this little baby single handed and I'll tell you what, in a rough sea she fucking don't go belly up." Lola was laughing and so was Shane and like he didn't know, Rob stood there. "What!"

Lola made some coffee in a small saucepan. It was still early enough for the sun to be like honey and they were sat on the rocks outside Rob and Lola's tent, relaxed as they could be. Lola had tied their tents flaps back and from where he was sitting, Shane could see inside. Near the back, almost covered in clothes, was a small blue Samsonite suitcase. The coffee was like liquid grit and if it had been anything but coffee, Shane would have thrown it away. They sipped it and shuddered as Rob laid out his plan. He sketched a rough grid of the site on the back of an opened-out envelope and said. "Way I see it, Lola and I take the detectors, she takes one half of the grid, I take the other. You follow us with a spade and dig up anything we buzz on. How does that sound?" It sounded simple but Shane didn't know. He had helped load and unloaded the 4x4 at the couple of hotels they had stayed at on the way from Madrid. He didn't remember seeing the suitcase before.

Pulling his mouth a bit to one side he nodded his head in agreement. There was nothing else to do now but something didn't sit right. Rob grinned at him and said. "Then when we've done that, we swop over to make sure we don't miss nothing, get it? That way we cover the whole fucking place, no problem. I reckon a day or two at the most." Shane nodded, he said. "How far does it go?" Rob said. "I told you it's state of the art. What?" Lola laughed again and Shane wanted to touch her and he licked his lips and Lola spoke. For a moment she looked straight at him and then she said. "Deep honey, Shane means deep. Like *treinta centímetros*, no?" Rob waved a hand at Lola, he said. "Yeh, yeh, I know we're all metric now but I'm a chap who doesn't like to convert."

To Shane he said. "It goes twelve to sixteen inches max." Lola said. "That's what I said, sweetie." Rob shook his head, pursed his lips and blew Lola a kiss off. "Nobody likes a fucking smartiepants, lovely." It was a joke too far for Lola, who smiled tightly and shook her head. Shane said. "That ain't very deep. What if there was a cellar?" Standing up, Rob took a drink of his coffee, pulled a face and threw the dregs into the undergrowth. Gesturing around him, he said. "See this here? This is practically flat, right? That house in the picture didn't have a cellar. Underneath whatever layer of topsoil is here it's got to be solid rock. Stands to reason! It's a fucking mountain ain't it? Fucking hell, you guys should watch a bit more daytime television, learn a few things. It's all out there guys." Rob picked up the metal detector again and started to look busy. Lola followed.

Shane sat where he was looking at the corner of the suitcase in the back of their tent and wondering. Lola glanced at him, followed Rob a few steps, then stopped and said. "Rob sweetie, I'm just going to get the sun lotion. You'll burn to bits if you spend all day out here, darling." Practically skipping over to Shane, Lola glanced quickly over her shoulder and seeing Rob still fiddling with the metal detector, kissed him on the lips. Quietly, she went. "mmmm." Her eyes were hard and stony and her skin shone like polished wood in the morning sun. Shane didn't try to touch her because he didn't know if he could stop and neither of them or Rob for that matter, were ready for that. Lola rubbed his chest through his T-shirt with the palm of her hand and went into the tent. Shane watched her. The way the material of her shorts tightened over her buttocks as she bent to enter the tent, the muscles in her thighs and calves as they moved with her. Crouched inside, she turned, shot Shane a brilliant smile of future promise and loosening the ties, let the flaps of the tent flop shut.

Several metres away Rob clapped the headphones over his ears, gave a shout of happiness and started careering around with his arms stretched out in front and the metal detector in his hands like it was out of control and dragging him here and there. He was going. "wehyhayhay." And. "Oooooo." The sounds seemed to bounce off the trees and the mountain and Shane wanted to slap him and have some silence back and he wanted to know what was in the Samsonite case. Soon Lola came out of the tent and tied the flaps back again. She gave Shane another look of promise and strolled away towards the manic Rob. The suntan lotion was in her hand and Shane couldn't help but admire her. Inside the tent the suitcase had been covered up.

Nothing happened. They worked the area methodically and Shane, shovel in-hand, loitered in a kind of no-mans-land between the two of them, waiting for the call. Once in a while the metal detectors went off and he dug holes. The metal detectors may have been set for gold and silver but all they found was bits of crap. Little oval, fake silver medallions with saints stamped on them. There were bits of locks and window latches, bottle tops, a couple of old pesetas and a tiny golden goat from a child's charm bracelet. Nothing they found even gave them hope. Rob always wanted him to dig deeper, bigger holes but there still wasn't anything to find. By mid-afternoon, it was job done. Neither Rob nor Lola really wanted to stop.

They crossed and re-crossed the whole open area where the house and car park had been, twice over. They backed up, fighting the undergrowth, to the slab of mountain at the back and all the way around the tree line and down the track almost as far as the boulder. Rob just couldn't believe it. He fiddled and tweaked at the metal detectors to no avail. He took the shovel and dug away at the holes until he struck rock. Lola followed him as he went from hole to hole and sifted through the bone-dry earth with her fingers, like they were looking for a lost wedding ring rather than a hidden golden hoard. They were both so intent, anyone watching would almost have thought they were for real. And Shane watched them, and wondered more about the suit-case than the family's lost hoard.

By four thirty in the afternoon Rob was prac-tically despondent. He couldn't think of anything else to do. The two metal detectors had been thrown aside and he'd given up the search. He knew love had his balls in a vice. He wanted Lola to love him. He wanted to give Lola something no-one else could. He wanted to give her the treasure. Now, sitting on a rock outside the tent, head in his hands like a broken man, he found it hard to accept failure. He wracked his brain for a new way to look at things. He knew he couldn't give up because Lola wasn't ready to give up.

She stood behind him rubbing his shoulders in that half-arsed way people do when they think they know how to give massages. Every once in a while he lifted his head and to nobody in particular, said. "Fuck sake!" Lola comforted him with kisses and plenty of honeys, darlings and sweeties. Shane didn't want to watch, he said. "Sixty odd years is a long time, maybe aunty was right and whoever burned the place down cleaned it out first." Lola wasn't having it and neither was Rob. In unison they shook their heads and said, emphatically. "No!" Lola's face had a nasty twist as she said. "That bitch! Fuck a duck! I'm happy that she's -." She stopped suddenly, blinked a couple of times and said firmly. "That woman kept everything. *No te daria ni el vapour de su meada*." Rob said. "Say what!" Shane said. "She reckons the old bird wouldn't give you the steam from her piss." Rob laughed.

Lola dug her fingers into Rob's shoulders until he winced and continued. "She ruined my father's life. It is here, I swear, I know it is still here. I've waited, I've waited so long for this-it's got to be here. I mean, it's here, I know it's here. This is the place, I'm not bonkers and by hook or by crook -. " Rob twisted himself to look at her and took her hand in his and Shane looked away. All Rob wanted to do was please her and he said. "Come on my lovely, I'm disappointed, so is Shane. Look lovely, if it's here we'll find it, I promise." It was an empty promise and they all knew it. But people choose to believe what they want. Rob looked imploringly at Shane. "Won't we Shane, won't we mate?" Shane didn't know, he would have liked to please Lola too but he didn't care the way Rob cared. He didn't like the mate stuff either but nodded anyway and glanced at Lola, who had come to Rob's side and squatted beside him with her head resting lightly on his shoulder.

Although she seemed fragile, almost close to tears, her voice was still firm as she demanded of Rob. "How?" Shane wondered if Lola ever really lost her head but he could see why Rob loved her so much. She gave Rob a self-confidence he'd never had before. She expected his support and she expected him to come up with answers. Somehow she'd helped him get out from under. For that she wanted ideas. Like metal detectors and now a plan B. For Lola there had to be a plan B. Shane didn't give a shit about plan B, just like he hadn't given a shit about plan A. He had his own ideas and none of them were based on trust of his companions. If he wanted to please Lola it was only enough to get close to her. If there was money to be had, he was interested. What he didn't want to do anymore was to watch these two fuckers pet each other.

Beginning to get his optimism back, Rob said. "We'll just have to have a fucking think, know what I mean? Reassess the plans. Fuck it, I mean like this stuff has been hidden for fucking years. This is only our first day, come on baby, chin up!" He chucked Lola gently under the chin. "Maybe I had the dials set wrong, eh?" Enough was enough. Shane stood up, he said. "I'm going to have a bit of a *siesta*. Give me a shout when you're ready to go for food."

He lay on the sleeping bag on his stomach, head near the open flaps of the tent. He wasn't sleepy. Ten minutes later he pulled himself quietly from the tent, closed the flaps and walked off through the scrub into the tall trees. A couple of paths for hikers came down off the mountain and Shane took the first one he came to. It was about wide enough for two people to walk side by side and followed the contours of the land up in a series of long zigzags. Every once in a while there was a sign fixed to a tree with a blazing fire crossed out on it. There were birds and bees and insects doing their thing. There was dappled sun and shade and sweet smells. Up above the trees, the sky was almost colourless and clear and crossed here and there by the spreading white slipstreams of jets already gone by. Shane walked through this idyll like a cynic, noticing only the plastic bottles and bags and bits of rubbish at the margins of the path. After about half an hour he came to an open escarpment with a bench chain-sawed from a fallen tree.

Shane sat on the bench and looked out over the wooded hills and mountains. He could see for miles. He could see towns and villages, roads snaking though the terrain and the flash as the sun caught the windscreens of passing cars and it went on and on until the world disappeared into the heat haze. There wasn't any wilderness anymore, not in Spain. There were no-camping signs, there were no-fire signs, there were park wardens and rangers. There were hundreds of hikers and walkers mooching through the mountains. So far they had been lucky. It had been about twenty four hours and he wondered how much longer they had before someone walked down off the mountain and discovered them. Or maybe that ugly git from the *Guardia Civil* would bother to drive up the track and arrest them for using metal detectors or taking something from the site that belonged to the King because even the rocks belonged to the King.

Sitting there he was wondering now, was she going to be worth it? There were always women if you wanted them. She was a package alright. He liked her body. He even liked the fact that she had an agenda beyond Rob or himself. He liked it that he didn't understand her. But was she worth it? He wanted to fuck her, have a laugh and a chat and maybe a few more fucks. It wasn't going to be a lifetime commitment. Sure there were times he'd wanted to be in love but these days he just didn't give a fuck. Maybe he was too cynical. Maybe he could only see the bad side of things. He'd seen plenty of people loved up but he hadn't often seen love repaid with love. Like with Rob, Shane didn't understand how after all the shit there had been in

Rob's life, he could still be so gullible.

He thought about the quiet of home and the nearby village and the people there who gave him smiles and treated him with respect and didn't know where he came from or what he was. If he left and went back now nothing would have changed and he could pick up that life and carry on. Trouble was he'd been sitting quiet and he didn't want to sit quiet anymore. There is always a moment to walk away clear from any situation but sometimes you can't help what you want. If love had Rob by the balls, boredom had him by the balls and Shane didn't kid himself, he was desperate for some excitement. Desperate to feel the blood rushing through his body like it had somewhere to go. After a while he walked back down to the tents.

The flaps were down and zippered up on Lola and Rob's tent and for a moment Shane wondered if they too had gone for a snooze and then he saw them coming towards him from the direction of the track. They were all smiles between each other and Rob had Lola pulled to him with an arm around her shoulder. Shane wanted. He didn't dislike Rob, at most he felt a bit sorry for him but he didn't have any real feelings about him at all. He was just a face from the past and a lot of people were now just faces from the past. He didn't give a fuck about Rob. Rob wasn't why he was there. Lola was.

They didn't see him until they were less than

ten feet away and like teens caught in the act, they loosened their grip on each other and Rob laughed in that way he had that made Shane want to smack him and said. "Alright geezer? Up and about! Yeh yeh." He did a little shuffle with his feet. Lola said. "Feel better after the snooze chap?" Rob said. "Yeh, it's been a hard fucking day for us all." Neither of them looked that upset anymore. Lola said. "Never mind, let's not be grouches, tomorrow is another day and all that mouth and trousers." Squatting on his haunches, Rob looked up at Shane and rubbed his hands together. "Maybe I was a bit fucking optimistic, know what I mean?" There was a nervous, slidey smile on his face and when Shane stared down at him, Rob blinked a couple of times and looked around and over his shoulder, as though expecting someone. Lola had gone in the tent and when she came out, she was carrying a wash bag and towel. She picked up one of the water containers and went behind the tent to wash. Shane sat on a rock opposite the open mouth of the tent. Inside it was neat and tidy and the Samsonite case was gone.

After a few minutes Lola came back looking all damp and luscious and went into the tent and dropped the flaps. Rob chuntered on in a virtual stream of consciousness about how he'd seen a programme on TV about these criminal gangs in Greece, who went to the sites of the partisan villages destroyed by the Germans in the Second World War. The Germans would bulldoze the villages and outlying houses and shoot most of the men and teenage boys. Many families had hidden their wealth, the way Lola's great grandparents had and quite often where it was hidden died with the men. People moved away or rebuilt the old village on a new site. The ruined villages were almost considered war graves. These criminal gangs, who the Greek police spokesperson maintained were usually Albanians, targeted a site and came mob handed, each with a metal detector and did a job on the place. "Yeh." He said. "That was where I got the idea for the metal detectors. See they took the cameras around one place that had been robbed and showed you all the uncovered holes where people hid stuff. Under the floors. In the walls. All sorts of places." He laughed. "Even under the shithouse! I thought fuck it, metal detectors, way to go! And concrete steps yeh, that was a favourite place. A lot of the steps were tiled and they'd build like fucking boxes inside the concrete so that when it's all fucking finished with the tiles and all that, everything looks fucking pukka." He picked up a handful of small stones and threw them at a bush. "Pity there ain't no steps here, eh?" Shane didn't answer him and Rob stopped talking as they both saw Lola emerging from the tent.

She didn't flaunt herself even if she knew she

looked good. She didn't sit down, either. She said. "Are we ready?" Smooth in a way that Shane had never imagined he could be, Rob rose and sidled up to Lola. He snaked an arm around her waist, he said. "Fucking hell! How did you manage to make yourself look so fucking good in a tent!" Lola was in a dark blue dress with a little pale yellow pattern on it that showed of her shoulders and arms, neck and legs and the walking boots with the rolled down socks just made her legs look longer and slimmer. There was no arguing with Lola. If Lola was ready, they were ready. They were going wherever Lola was going.

Where were they going? Rob had a map and they opened it and not wanting to meet the local *Guardia Civil*, fingered a large town about thirty K's away. Shane had been there a few times. He said nothing. It didn't bother him. Good seafood. Lola kissed Rob but she was looking at Shane. When they were done kissing, Rob said. "Hang on, hang on, explanations for Shane and all that! Look, today has been such a downer, we thought we should say fuck it and forget everything until tomorrow, know what I mean? We'll have some food, a bit of wine, fuck it, whatever's going, yeh?" He started fiddling about in the pockets of his shorts and pulled out his little box. He said. "A little something before we go?" There were still a few beans in the box and Rob took out three and handed them around.

The way Shane saw it, although he didn't really trust either Rob or Lola, he had nothing to lose, yet. There was too much at stake in his own life to be arrested for something stupid like illegal camping or those useless fucking metal detectors. If the *Guardia Civil* started to take a real interest he would cut and run or do whatever was needed to stay at liberty. It was simple. But clipping along in the 4x4, the little fella coming on through his body, nothing seemed to matter that much. He didn't even care that he was in the back seat alone or that Rob, next to Lola in the front, kept talking. He could see bits of Lola, her hands on the wheel, an arm, an ear, her neck and every once in a while her eyes, as she studied him in the rear view mirror. It wasn't enough but it didn't seem to matter right then. Something about the way she was gave him hope. The way she'd kept her eyes on him when she came out of the tent and even after Rob had kissed her, seemed to say that she had dressed for him. That's what he told himself, anyway.

6

They came into the town over a modern concrete bridge spanning a dry river bed and up a long narrow incline flanked by shuttered business premises, into a large oblong Plaza lined with dusty half-dead trees. They parked up and stepped out into a wonderful warm evening. But it was another nothing time in Spain, way too early to eat and way too late to siesta. They mooched about looking for a bar in which to loose a couple of hours. Most of the shops lining the Plaza were closed. The only ones open sold useless things like crockery, candlesticks, cloth flowers and plastic toys.

A few old guys sat talking and smoking on benches like they had been there forever. Little girls played skipping games. They chanted and ran in and out of the turning rope and in and out of the narrow streets and lanes that opened off the Plaza, teens on mopeds zipped about. It was a dreamy mixture. A kind of quiet that was never completely broken by the chanting, laughing girls and the slap of their feet as they jumped the rope, nor by the high pitched whine of the mopeds. The warmth of the evening, the smell of dust in the air, the occasional whiff or two of smoke all seemed to mix it up nicely so that it all belonged. Rob walked around with big eyes and a grin on his face. He took the air in like a dog with twitchy nostrils. Maybe it was the E but for once he seemed to have found something about Spain he liked. He said. "This is fucking lovely, init. Like out of a holiday programme or something." Lola playfully punched his shoulder and said. "It's Spain, my lovely. This is the real Spain." Yeh, Shane liked the town as well but he didn't tell them he'd been there before, with Jesus and now just hoped nobody recognized him.

They found a long thin bar full of men watching bullfighting on the TV and sat on bar stools drinking ice cold beer. The men covered every age men come in, but it was the old guys who were giving the chat to Lola and making her laugh. Shane didn't bother to translate for Rob, as one of the old men asked her who she was with and when she told them, laughed and said Rob wasn't much more than an old bit of boiled chicken neck and didn't she need a real man. One florid faced pensioner, the shape of a dumpling, patted his belly and told Lola she would be better off with a man with a bit of meat on the bone. Lola was easily able for them, giggling and wagging her finger and reminding them about their wives back in the house and maybe their wives would like any spare loving they had. The men nudged each other and laughed and then a fresh bull came running out into the arena and one of them grabbed a spare chair and motioned Lola over. Lola caught the barman's eye and ordered drinks and a round for the four old guys. She sat down at the table and the men were happy, happy to have a lovely young woman near them.

At the bar Rob and Shane tried to watch the bull fighting but it was alien and that bit of Spanish culture Shane couldn't come to terms with. Rob said. "Ain't this shit against EEC rules or something? Man it's harsh." At least he had the sense to speak quietly. Shane shrugged, he said. "Look somewhere else. Look at the bottles behind the bar." Shane looked away towards the bar's open door and out onto the Plaza. Almost directly opposite was another bar. There were tables under umbrellas outside and a scattering of customers. A black BMW pulled up just beyond the bar and two men got out. They stretched and looked about. One was English, London by the head on him, the other, younger, looked Spanish. They sat at a table under one of the umbrellas and ordered coffee.

Shane recognized the London head and looked about for another exit. There wasn't one.

Beside him, Rob said. "See, you have to try to get under the skin of people, think like they think, know what I mean? Like if I had a stash of gold why would I hide it in a house I thought was going to be burned down by a bunch of fucking revolutionaries? Everybody knows a fucking revolutionary needs either gold or diamonds. That's half the trouble. There was a fucking programme on the box, right, traced -." Shane turned on Rob. "What the fuck have you done?" Shane didn't mask the look in his eyes and Rob saw it and remembered the past. He choked a bit and glancing involuntarily down at Lola, said. "Nothing, nothing. What have I done? I ain't done nothing." Reaching across the space between their bar stools, Shane dropped his hand onto Rob's thigh and took hold of a handful of soft flesh. From the table, Lola said. "Alright chaps?" Shane turned and smiled. He looked at Rob, who didn't turn but gave Lola a little wave. With his free hand Shane got the barman's attention and ordered another round. There were tears in Rob's eyes. He tried to wriggle away, get off the barstool but Shane just made his fingers bite deeper and got close to Rob's ear and said. "The bog's down there, let's go." He made Rob go first but came up close behind, leaving a little wink and a grin for Lola. She smiled back.

The toilet was tiny, just enough space for three men pissing shoulder to shoulder. The two of them filled it quite enough. There was an aluminium trough set about crotch high, for pissing in. Rob was scared. He was pressed against a wall as far away from Shane as he could get. With a tremble in his voice, he said. "See, see, see these?" He pointed at the trough. "These are like a really bad modern invention, these, these fucking things are a backward step for mankind." Shane didn't want to hit Rob, he wanted Rob to tell him the truth. Rob swallowed and held one hand out in front of him as though it would stop Shane. "No really, see, see before, before you pissed in a little gully at your feet, right? Fuck it, worst thing that could happen right, was you got a bit of bounce back on your shoes, yeh? Now they move the fucking gully up to your thighs and call that fucking progress! Now the bounce back comes onto the front of your fucking trousers. How fucking hygienic is that, eh? Who thinks of these things, like who designs this fucking stuff, who -?" He stumbled to a halt.

Shane said. "What did you do to upset Dennis?" Although he didn't have anywhere to escape to, Rob looked around as though there could be a way out he hadn't noticed. In the end he gave Shane a pathetic glance and said. "Nothing. I, I, I don't know what you're on about, honest." That was it for Shane. Honest. The liars favourite word. He reached out and Rob tried to shrink back but he was already against the wall. Shane took one of his ears between his thumb and forefinger and twisted it until Rob was squealing and bending into the twist, until he had to grab hold of the urinal to stay on his feet. Shane said. "If you haven't done something to Dennis, why is the Cousin and some Spanish fucker sitting outside that bar across the square." To Rob it was like his ear was being ripped off but he'd had a lot of pain in his life and this, in real terms, was mild. He denied and denied and while Shane took it out on his earhole, Rob mostly thought about Lola and what they would do when this was all over. Nice stuff, happy ever after and all that. For the first time in his life everything was on the up and up and he wasn't going to blow it. There was no going back. Never ever.

If the Cousin was in Spain then they were definitely after him. Running into Shane and finding that he hadn't been sent to kill them was one of the best bits of luck they had had. Somehow Lola and he needed to find away of avoiding the thugs or turning Shane loose on them. Shane was beginning to really hurt him now but he wouldn't say a thing. He knew that sooner rather than later Shane would let go of his ear, they would go back to the bar and act naturally because Lola was there and Shane wanted Lola.

With a sigh, Shane released Rob's ear. What was

the point? He didn't need an explanation. The story was in the Samsonite suitcase. Fuck both of them. While he was still crouched by the urinal, Shane gave him a sharp kick in the thigh, just for being the annoying git he was. As he went out the door, he pointed at Rob's hand on the trough and said. "Make sure you wash your hands." Walking down the bar towards Lola, Shane had no idea what to do. Everything seemed to have changed. Any suspicions he had harboured were now made fact by the Cousin. There was a way out for Shane if wanted to take it. All he needed to do was itty over to the Cousin and his little helper and point the finger. Then he thought about the suitcase and how much cash could be inside. Also Lola looked amazingly beautiful sat in amongst the old Spanish geezers. Her head was tilted to one side and she was looking along the bar towards him with a soft, quizzical look on her face. Shane didn't know if it was for him or if she was wondering where Rob was. It didn't matter, Shane still wanted her. He smiled as though everything was rosy and said. "Rob's just washing his hands." Lola reached out and ran the tips of her fingers over the tips of his fingers and his whole arm tingled with pleasure. He sat on the bar stool and Lola dropped her hand and for a brief moment rested the palm on his knee.

Rob came out of the toilets then and Lola quickly took her hand away and gave him a little wave. Rob's hangdog face was pale, one ear was glowing and he had a slight limp. Taking a mouthful of beer, Shane watched from the corner of his eye as Lola, full of concern, jumped up to meet Rob. There were honeys and sweeties and darlings and kisses for his ear and Rob explained how, just as he was leaving the toilet he'd slipped on the wet floor. He said. "Yeh, I was just coming out and suddenly I went over, bang. I had the door open and somehow when I went down the door slammed shut on my ear. I mean, how fucking weird is that, eh? Chance in a fucking million or what?" Rob and Shane smiled at each other but Lola didn't believe a word. She looked from Shane to Rob and back again, she said. "I say chaps?" But Shane wasn't listening to Lola anymore. He turned away and looked over at the Cousin and his helper sitting like smug fucks on the other side of the square , almost like they knew they were there. He wanted to avoid them if he could, for all sorts of reasons.

For four years he'd kept out of everyone's way, perhaps even begun to think and feel like a changed person. Twisting Rob's ear was the most violent thing he'd done in all that time. But his history was always there even when he thought he'd put it behind him. Meeting Rob in Madrid should have told him that. Now it was like being with Rob and Lola had opened up a trail to the past. Something unseen had backed up and the shitheads were coming up out of the toilet bowl. They didn't want him right now but if Dennis knew where he was or that he was involved, it would change everything. Okay, he wanted excitement but he didn't want to have to kill anyone because he had a nice little bean buzz zapping at his heels and a cold beer in his hand. He wasn't looking for violence in any form but that didn't matter in the end, nor did the bean buzz. Not that much had changed really. What surprised Shane was that despite their lies and trickery he still preferred Lola and even Rob to the two fucks over the square because they knew where the money was.

When he looked back again, Lola was kissing Rob's ear and he had an arm around her waist. Shane sighed, it was time to find out what the fuck was going on. Rob said. "Oi, Lola lovely, Shane's got something to tell you." Snuggling up even closer to Rob and trying to look tough, Lola said. "No sweetie, first I have something to say." She paused and looked significantly at both men. She wagged her finger like someone's mother and said. "No fighting boys! We are supposed to be all friends here." Shane wasn't having it anymore, he said. "Fuck that." Lola looked aggrieved. Shane said. "We're not friends. Him and me, we were never friends and you? I know what you look like but I don't think I know who you are. Who are you?" Something hard came into Lola's eyes then and

Shane recognized it. It was the same look she'd had on her face when she was trying to get information out of the old aunty. Now it was focussed on him and it was true, he didn't know her. Pulling her closer, Rob said. "I think you better hear what he's got to say, lovely." The look didn't leave her eyes but she said nothing. Unable to contain himself, Rob said. "He knows, lovely."

Removing that penetrating gaze from Shane, Lola swivelled her head back to Rob and she didn't look so lovely now. "You stupid - stupid - you, you! Fuck a duck! I drag you out of the *mierda* - where would you be? Eh? Still going around making money for that *put*, Dennis? Stupid!" She waved a hand at Shane. "You want to trust this person? Didn't you hear him? He doesn't even like you. Why did you tell him! Stupid, stupid!" She wasn't quiet and the old guys she'd been sitting with looked over at Rob and Shane. They had serious heads on them as though anything they could do would make a difference but Lola had them content again in a second. She screwed a finger into the side of her head and in Spanish, told the old guys, Rob and Shane were brothers and you know how brothers are. *Loco. Siempre argumento.* Sometimes she just had to put them right.

The old guys nodded and looked around at one another because they all had families and they all knew it to be true. In a first attempt at Spanish,

Rob moved his hands in a calming wave and said. "*Tranquilo*, yeh? *Tranquilo*." The old men looked nonplussed and Shane caught the barman's eye and ordered brandies for the table and J&B's for Lola, Rob, and himself. They all clinked glasses and when everybody was almost friends again, Rob said, quietly. "I didn't tell him." Lola didn't believe a word but she didn't say anything. She stroked Rob's cheek. They looked at each other with little smiles, the way people do when they have an arrangement. Rob said. "He guessed." All softness and light again, Lola said. "It doesn't matter honey, nothing matters."

Shane was beginning to feel conned again. The idea that they had been working him together all the time was stronger than ever. They still knew more than he did. He looked at the loving, sweet talking couple and felt like putting a boot in their arses and kicking them out into the square. Instead he took Lola by the arm and took her to the door of the bar. Rob followed but hung back so he wouldn't be seen. Shane nodded over at the two across the square. "Do you know who they are?" Still playing umpty with Shane, Lola flared her nostrils, shook her head dismissively and tried to pull her arm away but he held her. "That English guy is Dennis's Cousin." Lola stopped pulling and let her body rest against his. Very quietly, she said. "Bugger." From behind, Rob said. "So, what do we do now? Does this mean the food's off, 'cause I'm fucking starving!" They both looked at Rob, he had a daft, ecstasy grin slapped on his face. Lola shook her head and in a despairing voice, said. "Honey, don't be a *limón*, not now."

They went back to the bar, ordered more drink and sat for a while buzzing and watching bulls being tortured. Not one of them knew what to do next. Rob and Lola were quiet, not talking or even looking at each other as reality began to bite. Sure they had imagined a situation where someone was sent to get them but actually seeing that someone fifty metres away, was something else. For some reason Lola sat closer now to Shane but let a reassuring hand rest on Rob's knee. Eventually Rob said. "So, what shall we do, sit here getting pissed and hope they go away?" Lola was scornful. "Is that the best you can come up with, sweetie? I thought you were the bees knees of ideas, honey." Rob rubbed his ear and then gingerly touched the bruise on his thigh. He looked around the bar the way he'd looked around the toilet earlier, as though there could be a way out he hadn't noticed. There wasn't.

He sighed, he wanted to put Lola right without upsetting her anymore and said, gently. "None of this needed to happen, so don't blame me. We're here because you want to find your treasure. I told you we don't fucking need it. We got so much fucking money we haven't even counted it. We pulled a stroke! For fuck sake we should have sidled off somewhere where nobody knows us, know what I mean, like? Not Spain but somewhere without fucking connections." He stopped talking, looked at Lola and Shane and said. "I ain't Shane's friend, I know that but I - I do sort of trust him. And you sweetie, you're lovely and gorgeous and I love you but you're a fucking dingbat! You got a one track mind. You want what you want, you're a determined dingbat! But sometimes we all have to take a fucking step back and look at the bigger picture." Shane started laughing and then Rob and Lola came in a grudging last. She pulled a face and said. "I don't like dingbat." Smooth as fuck, Rob kissed her neck, he said. "Don't get me wrong lovely, I want you to find that fucking inheritance because I know it's real to you, get me? I want you to be happy. But it ain't about no half arsed idea no more. It ain't just about what you want. We've got to decide about those fuckers out there. See, it's true, we could just sit here and get fucked and not go anywhere until after they've left but that wouldn't really get rid of them, would it? We fucking well know they're here now, don't we? We can't ignore it."

Shane knew he was a bit out of it but still it was strange hearing Rob talking sense or what seemed like sense. Another round of drinks came, sent by the old guys. Rob raised his glass to them and said. "*Gracias*." To Lola, he said. "So we give up on the treasure, yeh?" She didn't exactly agree nor did she disagree. Holding out his hand, Rob said, gently. "Here, give me that photo." Once again Lola took the picture out of her pocket book. They all looked at it. Rob took the snap and studied it closely, he said. "We weren't ever going to find anything with this, fuck sake, all you can really see is that big rock, the rest is just a blur." He held the picture between his thumbs and forefingers as though to tear it up. Lola grabbed it, she said. "No!" Rob said. "Come on lovely, what the fuck use is it? Let's leave the past behind, eh?" She looked at the photo for a long time, then ripped it into pieces and dropped the bits into an ashtray. Darting her eyes from Rob to Shane, she said. "We'll kill them." Rob tried to look shocked but it wasn't real. Half-heartedly, he said. "No, no, no." Then they both looked at Shane like it was time he started earning his money. It was what he was there for.

There was a silence. After a moment Rob shrugged and said. "What d'you reckon?" To Shane they were both smoozers. Here they were sidling up to him again, just the way they had on that first night. Nothing had changed but now he saw it all differently. Yeh, he still wanted to fuck Lola like when he saw her coming out of the crowd but now there was a suitcase full of money. He wanted her but not above getting the money. As far as Rob went, they say love has the ability to transform people and something in Rob had changed that was for sure. Now Shane was watching him. The truth was he didn't know what he reckoned on either of them anymore. To Rob and Lola, he said. "Just like that, eh? It's easy to talk about killing people but neither of you two know, do you?" Lola didn't answer. She shot a glance at Shane and stared down at her feet. Her fists were clenched. Rob gave a nervous little laugh and said. "It's them killing us I'm worried about." With a sigh and a shake of his head, Shane said. "This is some treasure hunt you pair of cunts."

7

Because they were ravenous and spending money, the barman made them ham and cheese *bocadillos* and when their blood sugar levels were back to normal, they all felt groovy again. The old guys decided to go back to their wives and Shane and the others moved to the table under the TV The bull fighting was over and some kind of luridly coloured soap flickered and burbled above their heads as they made a plan and agreed a split of the money. After a last J&B it was time to move.

Shane left first because they weren't looking for him and with the hair and the continental look, the fuckers wouldn't even notice him. A few steps from the bar there was one of the *callejóns* which intersected the square and Shane ambled down it, no hurry on him. Full night had fallen and everywhere was shadow dark with squares of light from windows and doors dropping like 3D, yellow and creamy, on the cobbles of the alley. All the disembodied sounds of living, the TVs, the radios, the pop music and all the people behind the doors and windows with all their chat, gently rolled around the alley, off the walls and over the cobbles and Shane rolled with it. Smiling and buzzing and now ready, no, wanting the action. Fuck it, boredom was like some yoke around your neck that you hadn't even noticed you were carrying until it was gone. Shane felt like he was growing. Halfway down the alley he took a right into an even narrower *callejón* and after a few yards exited onto the road that ran out of the town over the bridge. He walked back up towards the plaza and stood in the lee of a closed shop.

The 4x4 came around the corner slowly and stopped and Shane shot into the back, hugging the seat covers and they were moving again before the BMW came after them. But come after them it did. The car's headlights followed as they crossed the bridge and everything was right. On the open road speed limits were maintained and the BMW kept a discreet distance and although with all the drink, Lola must have been out of it, she drove like a sensible person. Rob cooed encouragement. Shane kept his head down. The miles slipped by, everything was set. But not, ofcourse and that was what Shane loved best, the fluid moments. Everything depended on what the two men in the car behind did next.

Lola went into the lay-by indicator flashing and stopped in the entrance of the track, so the car behind could see where they went as it cruised by. Shane got out of the vehicle and Rob and Lola kept on going up to the camp site. Before the other car returned Shane had chosen a spot for himself in the dry bed of the gully, running beside the track. He had the thick end of a heavy oak branch in his hand. He thought about the two men coming after them. If they drove up the track, he would follow the car and surprise them. If they walked, he intended to have them where he was.

The Spanish guy was of medium height, young and packed like he went to the gym. Shane didn't know him. But the Cousin had been around a long time. He was a big fuck, knocking fifty now and double hard, back in his day. He'd done most of Dennis's dirty work when they were coming up together. Not that either Dennis or the Cousin had to get their hands dirty in that way, anymore. Rob and Lola really must have pulled a stroke for Dennis to send out the Cousin. But Rob did say they had more money than they could count. Shane wanted to see inside that suitcase

He heard them long before he saw them. The Cousin was moaning because the Spanish guy wouldn't drive his car up the track. The Spanish guy was saying, your BMW we drive up, my BMW you walk, forget it brother. They kept telling each other to be quiet and tripping in holes, cursing the dark and asking why the other didn't bring a torch. The years sounded like they had taken a toll on the Cousin, who was wheezing up the steep slope like a pit pony. The Spanish guy had a shotgun under his arm as though out hunting and the Cousin was carrying a hand gun. Shane was there if you could see him and after they had passed he stepped out of the gully and smashed the oak branch into the back of the Spanish guy's head.

The cudgel thwacked into the soft flesh where the back of the skull meets the spine. The Spanish guy gasped, staggered forwards a few steps, fell to his knees as if he was about to vomit and slumped onto his side, half in and half out of the drainage gully. Then it was like slowmo'. Suddenly the Cousin was all alone in the dark, not knowing what had happened. He moved carefully towards the Spanish guy and crouching by him, called his name in a whisper. "Carlo! Carlo!" It took him maybe half a second to realize something was wrong. Quickly he straightened up and started to turn. By then Shane should have already hit him but he hadn't.

When he did it was too late and the blow bounced of the Cousin's shoulder before it hit his head. The branch broke on his brick thick skull and the Cousin staggered but he didn't go down. As he fought to stay upright he swung the gun and popped a nine. The explosion was orange and red and white and the bullet spun off, whining, into the trees. Shane threw himself at the man. It was like hitting a wall. The Cousin may have been getting old and bulky but he wasn't soft. They pushed and held, digging and thumping at each other, trying to hurt and looking for some kind of advantage. The Cousin was two inches taller than Shane and at least two stone heavier and he was handy. He knew the close up stuff the way Shane did. They grappled going for each other with short punches, hard digs and stamps, elbows and flashing foreheads and the clumping of the gun-butt into any part of Shane that the Cousin managed to get at. It wasn't going well and although Shane was more or less holding his own, he was getting hurt. The Cousin was big but he wasn't fit. He was already wheezing and just wanted to get far enough away to blow this cunt to bits. So they stumbled around like drunken friends until Shane's feet got entangled in the feet of the Spanish guy and he went over with the Cousin on top of him.

They were all in the ditch then. The Spanish guy was on the bottom. The shotgun was where it had fallen, cushioned on a bed of dry leaves, close to the Spanish guy's open hand but he was out of it. The Cousin was huge and heavy as he rose up above Shane, the gun free now and pointing straight at Shane's head. Shane saw the truth. There wasn't anything. There never had been. He had never believed that there was. Life was it. This was it and death was as good as anything else. All the desperate strength that had kept him alive down the years seemed to desert him now. He let his arms fall away from the Cousin and the Cousin held his head by the hair with one hand and the barrel of the gun was pushed into his forehead. The Cousin was looking down on him and in that moment Shane saw recognition kick in. The Cousin wrinkled his forehead, squinted and did a double take, he said. "Shane!" Then he smacked the butt of the gun into the side of Shane's head. He said. "What the fuck are you doing?" He hit Shane again. "Where are those cunts and where's the money?" He shook his head almost unable to believe who was underneath him and said. "Fuck you! What are you doing here! Fuck! Fuck! You in this? After all Dennis did for you, you cunt!" Shane thought he was going to pass out. His strength seemed to have abandoned him and couldn't seem to muster the will to do what he needed to do. He could see the shotgun and knew that if he struggled he could reach it. The Cousin hit him again.

Shane didn't like the idea that he had fainted but he had. He didn't see Lola suddenly hove into view and neither did the Cousin. To Shane it seemed she just materialized out of the dark or maybe he had just opened his eyes again. She swung the chopper Rob had insisted on bringing, even after Shane had told him they couldn't have camp fires and hacked into the side of the Cousin's face. His cheekbone gave a loud crack and a lump of flesh and skin flopped down to his chin. He grunted in pain, reared up and dropping Shane's head, tried to swing the gun around towards his attacker but Lola wasn't finished. With a Zena like scream, she chopped at his gun arm and Shane stretched instinctively for the shotgun. Lola hit him again on the head and Shane swung the shotgun up underneath the Cousin's jaw and gave him one barrel. Lola wailed like Gabrielle, dropped the hatchet and toppled over on her arse. The Cousin's head went everywhere and only the shotgun, like a prop, stopped the fucker's body falling completely onto Shane. He had been a heavy live cunt and now he was a heavy dead cunt and for some reason he wouldn't just fall away.

Maybe it was the Spanish guy beneath or maybe he was still weakened from his brush with death but Shane couldn't seem to get a purchase on the earth good enough to throw the Cousin off. Perhaps Shane would have liked to cry for a moment but he just didn't have it in him even though he felt weak and stupid and incapable. As it was Lola grabbed hold of the Cousin's shoulders and dragged the body partly off and Shane was able to pull himself out from under.

When he was on his feet, Lola said. "My God!" Relieved, Shane said. "Fucking hell!" He was alive. He gave a relieved laugh. Lola looked at him and gave a little shake of her head. Then, with a glance over her shoulder like she could see something in the dark, shot off up the lane. Quietly, as though it mattered, Shane said. "Lola?" But almost as soon as she'd gone, Lola was back. In her hand was a big rubber clad torch and when she turned it on it was so bright, Shane thought a spaceship had landed. There was gore everywhere, fragments of skull and brains in their hair, on their faces and clothes and blood like someone had thrown a tin of red paint up in the air. They looked each other up and down in silence and they looked at the Cousin's body and Shane came and stood beside Lola. He put his arm around her and she played the torch over the scene. The Spanish guy was still alive. His fingers searched surreptitiously for the shotgun. Shane walked three steps from Lola, picked up the Cousin's gun from where it had fallen on the path and gave the Spanish guy a cap for brains.

Putting the gun in the waistband of his shorts, Shane came back to stand beside Lola. She tilted her face up towards his and kissed him. Their faces were sticky and he could taste blood. She pulled the gun out of his shorts and dropped it into the dust.

As she kissed him she dragged at him and he went with her and they kind of wriggled to the ground and Lola put the torch beside the automatic. The torch light was garish all around them and full of looming shadows and Lola pulled Shane's shorts around his ankles and he grabbed the gusset of her knickers and pulled it to one side as she mounted him. Lola held his shoulders down and lowering her face to his, rubbed their sticky bloody faces together and shoved herself down on him. Shane could feel little bits of bone scratching at his face.

Neither one searched for subtlety. They were just fucking something out of their systems. It was a cunt and prick thing. They didn't think about how long it took. They didn't have time. Both were only interested in one thing. They wanted to be blown away for just that second. A blind whatever that wiped out everything. They fucked like there was no tomorrow and even if there was they still didn't give a fuck. When it was over, they lay laughing and panting on to their sides. They didn't have much to say because outside of the aftermath everything was wrong. Lola reached over and switched off the torch. They lay together in the strange, dark, silence and the dirt of the track was like a great big comfortable bed. They cuddled up close and enjoyed their moment in limbo.

Shane thought about the dead bodies and the BMW in the lay-by. He thought about Lola and why Rob had let her come back down to him on her own. Shane didn't know if it was love between Lola and Rob or what it was, perhaps mutual usage but they worked very well together. Whatever it was Rob was doing, it had to do with whatever he and Lola had just done and with the money and Shane could almost see Rob scuttling about the camp site looking for another new place to hide the suitcase. Lola was thinking too. After a while, she said, quietly. "My god, what's going happen? What will we do?" Equally as quietly, Shane said. "Nothing's going to happen. There ain't no-body near enough to give a shit."

Everything was clear to Shane now and for the first time in a while, he felt real. It could have been fucking Lola or the violence but his life was moving again. Extricating himself from Lola, Shane pulled up his shorts and went over to the body of the dead Spanish guy and took the car keys out of his trouser pockets. While he was there, Shane took his identity, all of his money and the spare shells for the shotgun. It felt good. He did the same for the Cousin, including the spare clip for the automatic. His pockets were full. He liked that. Lola had turned on the torch again and was sitting with her fingers in her hair trying to pull out bits of gore. Shane said. "Where's Rob?"

Lola stopped what she was doing and looked at Shane and Shane had the shotgun and he walked quickly over and picked up the automatic beside her. Although he wasn't pointing anything at her, Lola threw up her hands, jumped to her feet and for a moment, looked quite scared. The lovely little dress she was wearing was all ruffled up around her thighs and falling off one shoulder and despite the blood and dust she still looked pretty good. She tried to come the old innocent with Shane but when it didn't work, she joked and said. "Blimey, is this what we've come too? Holy mother of the beautiful God! We kill two people together, make wonderful love and this is what you ask me! Rob? Who? Who cares about Rob? Fuck a duck!"

Really she didn't seem that frightened to Shane and anyway, her and Rob worked like clocks, tic fucking toc. Then, almost as though she'd just hit reality checkpoint, she said. "Gosh! Golly! Are you going to kill me now?" Her hands were dangling by her sides and she didn't bother to try to right her dress. She looked like a pathetic porno schoolgirl. Shane didn't lie to himself, he wanted her again. Maybe not at that moment but again, like despite the bullshit, he hadn't had enough yet. When Shane didn't kill her, she said. "Rob told me you could take care of yourself." Lola's lips made a little moo, like she was innocent and had never once in her life taken hacks out of someone with a hatchet. She made a half-hearted attempt to straighten her clothes.

Why would he want to kill her? For Shane it was simple, he hadn't got his share of the money yet. She pulled up the errant shoulder strap of her dress and tugged a bit at the hem but nothing really happened. The shoulder strap slipped back down again. Even though he could see through her act, he still liked it a bit, he said. "You saved my life." That much was true. There wasn't anything more he could say. They stood and looked at each other. He shrugged and although he didn't trust her, he stuck the handgun into the waistband of his shorts and handed her the shotgun. Lola held the weapon for a moment, it was sticky with blood and dust and wrinkling her nose, she rested it against a bush.

Shane left Lola with the bodies and went down the track to get the BMW. While he walked he thought about the money, he thought about Lola's body and he thought about the past. It was true what the Cousin had said. Dennis had done a lot for Shane down the years. He wouldn't be a free man now without Dennis's connections, and if Dennis ever found out about the Cousin, he'd be a dead man. But he wasn't, not at that moment. It was all there was. All there ever was. And he thought, fuck it! Nothing mattered. He was still alive. He was walking through a wonderfully warm night full of the smells of the forest and he didn't know what was going to happen next. What else was there? It was like he'd been living behind glass for the last four years and now it was shattered.

8

The low slung BMW didn't like the track and even though Shane guided it as carefully as he could over the potholes and rocks, the arse end clattered and scraped. Lola was sitting near the bodies, the shotgun at her feet. She raised an arm to cover her eyes as the car lights threw the scene into garish relief. She looked unhappy and vulnerable and perhaps she'd even been crying. Shane unlocked the boot and said. "You alright?" Coming to the back of the car, Lola put her arms around his waist and resting her head on his chest, said. "I feel a little bit up shit creek, honey." She was all warm up against him and it took all his strength to remember that regardless, they weren't in this together. Yet he still held her for a little while. Eventually, Lola said. "Okey dokey."

There were two bags in the back of the car. The

Cousins bag had shaving things, a few clothes and in a side pocket, a clear plastic bag with about two grand in nice new twenty and fifty pound notes. Somehow Shane managed to find room for it in his bulging pockets. The Spanish guy's bag had more clothes and box half full of shells for the shotgun. His shorts wouldn't take anymore. Shane emptied the Cousin's clothes into the bottom of the boot and put the shells and everything in his pockets into the bag and tossed it onto the backseat of the car. Flatly, Lola said. "Are you collecting for charity?" Shane said. "Money's money."

He opened the front passenger door and pointed to the seat. But Lola wouldn't get in, she shook her head and waved her hand at the two bodies, she said. "No honey, when we've moved those." The two guys were dead meat and heavy. Shane let her help. They dragged the two bodies, one by one over to the car. The way Lola got her body weight under the Cousin as they heaved him into the boot was impressive and Shane told her so. She shrugged, she said. "I worked in an old people's home, remember? Believe me honey, they may be alive but some of them are heavy like they are already dead."

When they were finished and sat in the car, Lola turned the rear-view mirror towards her and studied herself. By the way she scowled, the prognosis wasn't good. To herself she said. "Okey dokey." She tried pulling more stuff out of her hair but it had mostly dried and all mixed up with dust and after a minute or so she sighed and flopped back in the seat. Before they set off, she said. "Please, don't tell Rob." Shane nodded but to his way of thinking, Rob already knew. Surely it was part of the deal the pair of them had. As for Lola, even if Rob didn't know, she would do almost anything to get what she wanted. Shane didn't know what to make of her. They had killed together and fucked together but other than the bits he wanted, she was a mystery to him. One thing he knew, he didn't want anyone like her looking after him when he was old.

They crept up the track in first gear, the front end of the car high from the extra weight in the boot and wallowing in and out of the potholes, while the rear end bumped and scraped on every ridge and rock. It was slow going. When they were near the big rock, Rob stepped out from the undergrowth into the headlights. Shane wondered how he knew it wasn't the Cousin and his helper. Had he followed Lola down the track? Had he watched them?

There was a big grin slapped on Rob's face and he rubbed his hands together. As Shane rolled down the window, he said. "Fuckin' hell, am I glad to see you! You been gone so long I thought you'd fucked off and left me again, then I thought, no fucking way, I'm the only one who knows where the money is." He laughed like it was a joke but it wasn't. Lola's face was like stone but she spoke softly to Rob. "Sweetie, I'm tired, I need to wash lovely, can we just move on and chit chat later?" Rob ducked down and peered into the car's interior. Lola looked at him with large black eyes that told him nothing. He nodded and said. "Yeh, yeh, you look well fucked my lovely, like you been in some kind of bloody tussle, know what I mean?" Lola managed a wacked out smile and mumbled. "Don't worry, lovely, we cut the custard, we can relax soon." Shane put the car in gear and drove it bumping up the last stretch of track onto the small *mesa* and parked it next to the 4x4. Before they climbed out, Lola said. "Maybe I've been a *limón*."

Rob certainly didn't seem surprised by the two bodies in the boot. In his minds eye Shane again saw Lola run off up the track and come back with the torch. Maybe they had both been lemons. Rob was a survivor. He'd been used and abused by people like Shane for years, to the point where nobody noticed they needed him. Although Shane had realized Rob had changed, he just hadn't seen how much. Now only Rob knew where the money was and Shane didn't think even Lola had seen that coming. Yeh, people had needed Rob for whatever and now they needed him. That was what made him a survivor.

The three of them stood looking into the boot.

It wasn't pretty. Rob whistled and said. "You made a fucking mess of them." Lola said. "I need to wash." Shane said. "Me too and we need to talk, we can't stay here." This seemed to please Rob, who began rubbing his hands together again and grinning. He said. "Yeh, yeh, it's all happening. Pity about them two but every fucking cloud and all that, yeh? Wait 'til I tell you."

The other two looked at him like they'd never heard of silver linings. Lola said. "Honey, I just helped kill -." Rob nodded quickly a couple of times, he said. "That's what I'm trying to say, lovely. If -." Shane slammed the lid of the boot shut. Lola said. "Fuck a duck Rob, there's blood in my hair!" He touched her hair, he just loved her so much, even when she treated him like shit, he said. "Alright, alright, yeh, yeh, I, I'll tell you later." Nevertheless he looked crestfallen and went to turn away, stopped, sniffed the air and said. "Is that petrol or what?"

They all sniffed. It was petrol. Rob got on his knees and felt around under the car. After a few seconds he stood up and held out his hand. It was slick with fuel. Shane got the torch from inside the car and they all looked underneath. Sure enough there was a slow drip of petrol coming from one corner of the fuel tank, where it had been punctured bumping up the track. They needed the car running. They couldn't leave it on the mountain. If the cops came back after they had gone and found the BMW, how long would it take them to trace the 4x4? They already had Lola's details. No, as far as Shane was concerned, they had to clear out before morning and dump the BMW somewhere well away.

Rob nipped over to their tent and came back all pleased with himself, like a little boy after his first successful solo trip to the corner shop. In his hand was one of their two saucepans. Getting down on his knees, he slid it under the drip. Back on his feet, Rob made a gesture with both his hands like a magician after a trick and said. "Problem solved! When it's full we'll pour it back in the tank." Shane couldn't understand how Rob was in such a good mood still. Couldn't he see that neither he nor Lola would be happy until they could get next to the suitcase.

By Rob and Lola's tent, Rob lit all three of the gas lamps they had and hung them from the bushes. Shane and Lola stripped down to their underwear and Rob poured water over them from a 5 litre plastic container, while they rubbed shampoo in their hair and soaped their bodies. Rob was buoyant, humming an old Frank Sinatra song about how the best was yet to come. He pointed at them and laughed and told them how he'd seen a discussion programme on the TV about whether life reflected art or art reflected life. He laughed, he said. "Because this is like fucking Pulp Fiction, know what I mean? Like life is reflecting fucking art, yeh? The fuckers on TV reckoned it wasn't one thing or another but like a chicken and egg thing. I couldn't see it at the time but like I'm fucking getting it now! Like who knows how many people have done this shit before Tarentino stuck it in a movie, right?" He shook his head, laughed again and poured more water over them until they were rinsed off and then wagged a finger at them and in a mumsey type voice, said. "Now put on some clean clothes and don't you dare come home that dirty again." Neither Lola nor Shane laughed. Nor had they looked at each other as they washed and dried themselves off. Something may have been unfinished between them in Shane's mind but it was as though nothing had ever happened either.

Both of them were now thinking of Rob and what he'd done with the money and how to get their share. Lola had ways of getting what she wanted and Shane had other ways but they were both weary. On the other hand, Rob was like someone who didn't know when the fun was over. When they had finished cleaning themselves up Rob put a saucepan of water on the little cooker and set about making some coffee.

They had things to talk about and Rob was strangely keen but not to talk about the suitcase. Both Shane and Lola tried. Shane mentioned the need to get rid of the car. Lola talked about how the family's lost gold could stay lost because this wasn't a happy place and anyway they had money. More than once he said. "Alright we got a couple of dead geezers in a car but it ain't all doom and gloom, come on, every fucking cloud and all that, yeh?" Lola tried giving him the lovelies and sweeties as usual but there was a tired, cynical twist to her mouth as she spoke and when Rob tried to kiss her and say whatever it was he wanted to say, she turned her head and said. "I'm going to rest in the tent sweetie, call me when the coffee is ready." Pulling his head down into his shoulders like a tortoise withdrawing into his shell, Rob rubbed his nose, gave Shane a perplexed look and said. "Don't neither of you want to hear what I've got to say?" Shane looked straight back at him, turned and walked away.

Shane felt as if he was there on his own. He got the guns from the car and the bag with the shells, passports and money and took the stuff over to his tent, along with one of the lamps. As he passed, Rob was on his knees, arse sticking out of their tent, whispering to Lola. Outside his own tent, Shane tipped the contents of the bag into the wavering halo of gas light. First he reloaded the guns. Then he got all the cash and bringing out his rucksack from the tent, zippered it safely into a side pocket. He was tempted to keep the Passport and IDs, knowing his friend Jesus would be able to shift the lot to connections in Granada. In the end he didn't want anything to come back to him, nomatter how slim the chance. He got the shovel and buried the lot in one of the holes he'd dug earlier in the day.

He wasn't sentimental but he couldn't help flicking through the Cousin's passport before it went into the hole and had to smile when he noticed it wasn't in his real name, which was the same as Dennis's name and which was why he was the Cousin. Most people didn't realise that they weren't even related. They had met in some kind of juvenile detention centre. The Cousin smacked down some teenage twat with beef for Dennis and a lasting bond was formed. When they got out they stuck together. They'd both had had long careers. Dennis knew how to use people. Dennis was vicious and smart. The Cousin had been a fighter but that didn't make him dumb. He had been more than just a thug with half a brain. Survival demanded it.

Shane and the Cousin had done a few things together when Dennis had first taken Shane under his wing. He hadn't wanted to kill the Cousin. It was just the way it happened. It could as easily have been the other way around. What he didn't want was Dennis finding out. Rob and Lola were travelling on their own passports, the car was hired in

Lola's name and he could see now how easy they had been to find. So far they were all Dennis was looking for. Oh yeh, them and the money. He hoped when the Cousin didn't come back, Dennis would let it go because for sure, if he looked hard enough he would find Shane.

After he'd finished burying the papers, he rolled up his sleeping bag and began to take the tent down. He emptied his rucksack of clothes, to make way for money and spread them out on the tent before packing that away. He was ready to leave and ready to talk about the cash. Turning from the packing to pick up the guns, he saw the wavering light of a gas lantern moving towards the track. Fuck them!

Grabbing the handgun, he shoved it down the back of his jeans and set off after the light. It had been Dennis who had really given Shane his start. Bringing him on, trusting him when he was still in his teens. Backing him for the first couple of big ecstasy buys. Sure, when the bean thing really took off they had both made a lot of money and Shane and Dennis were like Siamese twins for a while. Even when they had stopped working together they had stayed close. Fingers in pies and all that. It was Dennis who had organized Shane's escape from England on the trawler, four years earlier. Apart from Gerry his childhood friend, Dennis was one of the only people he really missed. Killing the

Cousin would fuck things up.

As he got closer, Shane could hear the mumble of their voices and see the light of the lamp, off the track, up by the side of the big rock. Suddenly Lola gave an excited squeal and Rob said. "See I told you, didn't I." Then almost reverentially, Lola said. "Holy Mother of the beautiful night." When Shane pushed through the bushes and up by the side of the big rock, they were both on their knees and neither seemed all that surprised to see him. They turned big eyes on him and Rob raised the lantern. He looked about as happy as Shane had ever seen him, he said. "Here Shane, come and look at this." Both had neat 100 gram ingots of gold in the palms of their hands. "This is what I was trying to tell you over by the tent."

They were kneeling beside a hole about 200mm by 300mm, hewn from the solid rock hard up by the side of the big boulder. Rob motioned Shane down beside them. As he knelt, Lola reached into the hole and lifted out another three small gold bars and fanned them out in her hands, towards him, like playing cards. It could have been the gas light but to Shane, Lola's face seemed to radiate a beatific glow. Maybe it was pure greed shining through. Either that or her eyes were luminous with unspilt tears. Whatever the emotion, it was real to Lola. Carefully she laid the small gold bars on the ground. Looking from one man to another

Lola began to grin. She spread her arms wide and hooking a hand around each mans neck drew them roughly towards her until all their heads clunked together and plopped a big wet kiss on each of their cheeks. She held them there in a tight little embrace for a few moments and when she released them, the tears were rolling down her cheeks but she looked almost transcendentally happy.

She said. "Golly gosh chaps, this really is the bees knees! You don't know - you just don't know what this means to me. It's like my whole life was for this. It wasn't all mouth and trousers. I was right." She lifted her chin and her smile hardened for a moment, she said. "All the past things, blimey, nothing matters now, does it?" Rob ran his hand over her arm and said. "Nothing matters now, sweetie. Don't think about those men. It was them or us." Lola stroked a bar of gold with her finger tips and said. "I wasn't thinking about them."

Shane picked up one of the gold ingots and held it close to the lamp. It didn't glitter. The surface was dull and dark, almost a coppery colour but there was no mistaking what it was. Nevertheless, taking the BMW keys from his pocket, he scraped the bar until a thin scar of yellow glittered in the light. Rob and Lola were reaching into the hidey-hole one after the other and pulling out a few bars at a time. There were twenty. There was also an oil-cloth bag full of useless, large denomination, old

Peseta notes as big as man-size tissues. Rob seemed to like the colourful paper money as much as the gold and scrutinized the huge bank notes, not wanting to believe they were useless. Taking a modern 100 *Peseta* note out of his pocket, he placed it beside one of the old notes, he said. "Fuck it, don't modern money make you feel like we're being ripped off, know what I fucking mean? At least this old stuff looks like it was worth something. Look at it." He picked up one of the largest notes and waved it about. "Imagine slapping that on the bar for a couple of beers." Lola looked at him and shook her head. Rob grinned and said. "What?" Plucking the note from between his fingers, Lola picked up the rest of the *Pesetas* and stuffed the lot into the bag and dropped it back into the hidey-hole. Smiling, she said. "Honey, let's leave this crap for some other *limóns* to find." She crumpled one in her hand. "No good to spend and too harsh for the bottom." They laughed together. Rob was happy. He'd done it. He'd found the treasure against all the odds and Lola was happy.

Shane liked to see people happy and in love but not up that close, not after what had happened. Yeh, he was glad they were happy. They deserved each other. Anyway he wanted to be gone. Wanted to dump the BMW and the bodies and be on his way. Fuck the gold. He'd have to go to Morocco, to get rid of it safely. Shane liked cash. He said.

"Where's the case?" Both Rob and Lola looked at him but their looks were different. It was as though Lola was coming back from a dream to reality and she blinked and immediately swung her gaze to Rob. She wasn't smiling anymore. To Shane the suitcase was worth much more than the gold. Rob scrunched up his face as though he'd been poked in the eye. He seemed confused, not guilty or worried, more like his integrity had been questioned and everybody likes to think they have integrity.

Once again, Shane said. "Where's the case?" Rob picked up the 100 *Peseta* note off the ground and shook his head. "Fuck me! What are we, eh? I thought we were in this together." Folding the hundred, he stuck it in a back pocket. Lola tried to speak but hurt, Rob cut across her, he said. "Yeh, you an' all." He shrugged and rubbed his nose with his knuckles and said. "All you're interested in is the money and the gold. You haven't even asked me how I found your treasure. And you Shane, fuck it man, you saw me come down by the side of this fucking rock. How far away do you think the fucking case is?" Shane took out the gun. He didn't point it at anyone. A metal detector was propped up against the rock. Shane said. "You found it with a metal detector, it's over there." Rob gave him a hurt look, reached into the nearest bush and pulled out the suitcase. Lola gave a relieved sigh. Rob put the case on the ground between them, flipped the catches and said. "There! Satisfied!"

Shane and Lola looked in the open case. Dismally, Rob said. "You know what? This reminds me of this film I saw on the telly when I was a kid. Old fucking thing. Humphrey Bogart was in it. Can't remember what it was called like but these three guys go off up some mountain in fucking Mexico or some fucking place, prospecting for gold. Everything's alright until they find the gold. Fuck it man, those cunts ended up so fucking paranoid they were trying to kill each other. Humphrey Bogart was amazing, totally mental! But that's not the point. Fuck it, we've got what we came for, can't we just trust each other now, just for a little while?" He held out his arms but when he saw the blank looks on Shane and Lola's faces, he let them flop to his sides. The case was full of good English money. Maybe Rob was sincere but Shane just wasn't in a very trusting mood, he said. "I want a third of what's in the suitcase. That's what we agreed in the bar."

The three of them looked at each other, and again stared down into the open case. The money wasn't in neat bundles, the way it always is in the movies but in a higgledy-piggledy mess of mixed up denominations. Mostly fifties and twenties. The small case was so full now that it was open, a couple of twenties fluttered to the ground. Picking up the notes, Lola put them back on top of the rest and pushed the whole pile down but it wouldn't stay compressed. Shane said. "Give me what we agreed and I'll take the BMW and dump it and the bodies. We can all be gone in half an hour and we never have to see each other again." Lola said. "A third? We don't even know how much is here."

It was in Lola's eyes and Shane could see it. She didn't want to share. She wanted the lot. One hand rested on top of the cash, keeping it in place. The other unconsciously stroked a gold bar. Rob frowned like he didn't want any trouble and said. "Shane's right. We should give him what we agreed and we should all fuck off. If he's going to get rid of the bodies great! Let's all just disappear. Fuck it Lola, come on!" But Lola didn't want too. She tried to look fierce, she said. "You agreed. In Madrid, you agreed, not me." Shane stood up beside Rob. It wasn't anything. His knees hurt from squatting. Looking up at them, Lola said. "The big man with the gun stands up. Am I the fly in the jam? Is that it?" Rob said. "We agreed in the bar. We shook hands on it." Half crouched over the money and the gold the way she was, Lola looked small and vulnerable to Shane. He didn't want to hurt her. He stuck the gun into the back of his jeans. He said. "Look, we need something to carry the gold in. I'll go get us a rucksack or something."

Shane wanted to leave them alone. He wanted Rob to talk a bit of sense into the lovely Lola. Even a compromise would do. For Shane nothing was ever set in stone. Nothing ever could be. Also he felt the desperate need to be gone. But not empty handed. He looked at them both. Lost for words for once, Rob's hands were in his pockets and his shoulders hunched. As for Lola, she was stone faced, eyes on Rob, on Shane and she wasn't going to let anything slip by her. She didn't trust anybody. Anything outside of her immediate greed, like the dead bodies, did not register anymore. Shane turned to go. Lola sprang up, shoved him and as he stumbled, managed to wrench the gun from his jeans. Shane fell against the rock and Lola backed off to the money, gun pointing at him. Hands out of his pockets now, Rob waggled them about and jumped between them. "Woa! Hang on! Hang on!" Lola shut the case, she said. "Remember, I can kill people too, big man."

Believing he had sway with Lola, Rob didn't move when she asked him to stand aside. He stopped waving his arms and in a serious voice, said. "Like I told you earlier, lovely, you're a fucking dingbat. Ain't we done enough already? Ain't there enough dead bodies?" Moving the gun slightly so it covered both the men, she said. "Don't dingbat me. I told you I don't like dingbat." Rob nodded his head, he said. "Alright, alright." Shane rested back against the rock and waited. Lola said. "Why should I share? This gold is mine by right."

Giving the case a kick, she continued. "And this? Sweetie, lovely, darling, ducks, you are as you say, a fucking muppet. Without me you would still be running around for that man Dennis. You should pay me for giving you such an interesting *las vacaciones*. You are a good, harmless man. I don't want to kill you but I will. Don't force me. If you help me, I'll give you some money of course but not him. I owe him nothing."

Rob had been fucked over many, many times in his life but this was probably the harshest. He could stand being beaten by people he didn't care a fuck about. He could stand being ripped off. It was part of the trade he'd been in. To be called harmless by the woman he loved, that hurt. To realize all he was worth to her was a few bob to keep him on side, hurt too. For a few moments in time, back when he'd handed Lola the first gold bar and seen the look of wonder on her face, he thought he'd got it made. If anything made her love him, the way he loved her, it should have been finding the gold. Rob glanced helplessly over his shoulder at Shane. Shane said. "So you were going to tell us, how did you find the gold?" Rob couldn't help himself, he moved slightly, to point at the cavity in the rock. Lola's eyes flicked and Shane kicked Rob hard in the back.

Almost before Rob had fallen into Lola, Shane was on top of her. Lola wasn't ever going to be quick enough with the gun and it was out of her hand before the sheer weight of the two men carried her to the ground. She screamed and kicked and Rob rolled off her because despite everything, he didn't want to hurt her. Shane didn't care anymore. He gave her a smart tolchock to the temple and her body slumped beneath him. On the ground beside her, Rob stroked her cheek with one hand and held the small of his back with the other. He said. "She wouldn't have hurt you, not really." Having seen her hack away at the Cousin, Shane wasn't so sure, he said. "I'll go and get something to carry the gold."

The ideas man in Rob wasn't home. Looking up pathetically at Shane, he said. "What'll we do now?" Shane wanted to kick him again, instead, he said. "I know what I'm doing. I'm pissing off. You two can do what the fuck you like as long as you stay away from me." He pointed at the prone Lola. "She'll be awake by the time I get back, talk some sense into her."

Before he got his rucksack, he checked the saucepan under the petrol tank of the BMW. It was almost full. He unlocked the petrol cap and carefully poured as much of it as he could, back into the tank. Things weren't going right. But then it had been wrong from the start and he'd more or less known it. A part of him wanted to say fuck the money, another part of him wanted it all. He put the saucepan back under the car and went over to the 4x4. Maybe the keys were inside. No. The 4x4 was locked up tight. Had the keys been in the ignition maybe he would have just gone but they weren't. A lantern was still burning near Rob and Lola's tent, as was the gas stove. The forgotten coffee had burned dry and the enamel on the pot was crackling with the heat. He turned off the stove. From his own spot he collected the camping gear, the shotgun and shells and left it all, except for the rucksack, near Lola and Rob's tent.

This time he was quiet and careful as he came up by the side of the big rock. As he got close he could hear the low murmur of Rob's voice. Shane had the gun out. It wasn't necessary. They were sitting side by side and Rob had an arm around Lola's shoulder. When Shane came through the thin bushes with the gun levelled at them, Lola still had a stunned look to her. She flinched. Rob stopped talking. Shane said. "Well?" It would have been easy now. Take the 4x4's keys from Lola. Put the gold in the rucksack. Give them both one in the head. Pick up the case and the rucksack and drive away. Who came up here beside the rock? Nobody. If they did, the gold would have been found years ago. In a month or so all the furry critters living in the woods and the crows, the ants and the wasps would have about picked the corpses into an unrecognizable state. Human bones and a bit of rotted flesh would be all that was left. Only their teeth would tell a tale. That was if anybody ever found their remains.

9

Rob rose slowly to his feet as he saw Shane come up to them with the gun. He said. "No, no, Shane, no." His eyes were full of fear and Lola looked down to the ground as though waiting for the worst. Shane didn't want to kill them, he said. "You know that film you were on about. Those guys in Mexico. What happened?" Rob glanced down at Lola, something had changed and Shane could see it. True Rob had calmed her down but now, before he answered Shane, he sidled away a couple of nifty steps and eased himself up against the rock. Maybe he'd decided he wasn't going to die for love. From the ground Lola watched Rob and it hurt her. Under her breath she said. "*Puta*." Rob didn't let the insult get to him, too much. As quietly as Lola's, "*Puta*", Rob said, sadly. "Lola." It seemed to Shane that Rob didn't trust his lovely Lola anymore. He dropped the rucksack in front of Lola and said. "Put the gold in there." Without argument Lola pulled herself onto her knees and began to put the gold slowly into the bag. Rob said. "I think Humphrey Bogart got killed by some bandits and all the fucking gold dust blew away in a sand storm. There was this famous line, people still quote it but I can't remember what it is." Shane said "Lucky this ain't dust."

When the gold was in the rucksack, Shane took the suitcase in his free hand and waved the gun at Rob, he said. "Get the rucksack." Even if Rob didn't trust Lola anymore, he still had feelings for her. He wasn't sure what those feelings were but whatever, he didn't want her dead. Gingerly moving away from the rock, he shifted his hands about in front of him and rolled his shoulders in a hopeless kind of way but he didn't pick up the bag, he said. "Can we, can we stop, like. Can we just stop for a minute? Please? Can't we talk about this one more time? Please?" On her knees still, Lola looked from man to man. For the first time in a long time, she felt beaten, powerless. Everything she had strived for was right in front of her. Somehow though, none of it was hers anymore. Not even her life. Everything had been taken out of her hands and she didn't like it. Lola believed people had preyed on her until she had learned to prey on them. Yet here she was. To get to this point in her life Lola had done things that disgusted her more than murder but now she didn't have anything left. She didn't know how to change the situation. Already she'd had to agree with Rob to share the money. She didn't like that either but she wanted to live.

Now on her knees, with two dickheads about to decide her fate, her chest was so tight she could barely breathe. She didn't know what to do but wait. She didn't dare move a muscle but she searched her brain for a way out. She felt very close to her death. Useless ideas zapped though her mind, like acid flashbacks. The world became a small place. Her vision narrowed until the mountain, the two men, the money, the gold, the very ground she knelt upon coned into the narrow end and all she could see was a patch of weeds and the corner of the rucksack. It was almost too real. She waited.

Rob couldn't help defending her, he said. "You don't understand. This gold is all she's thought about for years. Fuck it, don't kill her. She made a mistake. It was emotional. Family stuff, you know? She just got over excited. Fuck it yeh, she's sorry, she told me. Yeh like, really sorry." He waved a hand towards Lola. "Look, she's on her fucking knees, man." Shane didn't care. He could get a blow job anywhere. Anyway from where Shane was standing Lola didn't look up to it. He reached down and pulled her to her feet. To Rob, he said.

"Get the rucksack." Shane held the lantern high and pushed the pair of them through the bushes and onto the track. Nobody was arguing anymore. They trudged back to the camp Indian fashion, Shane at the rear. As they neared the tent, Rob said. "At least that coffee should be ready." Shane couldn't help sighing. Like they were good mates on the way back from the pub, Rob called back. "I know mate, little bit of caffeine, do us all the world of good. Help us think."

The coffee was a thick, black glaze in the bottom of the saucepan and the saucepan was fucked but to Rob it was like his favourite granny had died. He clapped his hands around his head, elbows tight in like a boxers and wailed. "Fuck sake!" He plonked himself down on a rock and went all limp for a moment. Lola let herself sink onto another rock and looked at the ground. Shane smacked Rob around the back of the head with the gun butt and Rob let him pull the rucksack off his back. Miserably, Rob said. "Don't hit me again. I've had enough of being hit. People have been bullying me all my life. You all think I'm fucking stupid but I ain't. That fucking gold would still be lost if it wasn't for me. If you want to kill me get on with it or leave me alone." The fucked saucepan was still sitting on the top of the little stove. Rob picked it up and getting to his feet, hurled it into the undergrowth before sitting back down again. He said. "I was fucking looking forward to that coffee."

Shane wanted to hit Rob just to shut him up but ignored him instead and stepped over to Lola. Mixed up between fear and anger, Lola couldn't bring herself to look at Shane because she didn't know what she might do next. Like Rob, if he was going to kill her, she wanted it over with. He stood there for perhaps half a minute, waiting for her to acknowledge him then dropped the rucksack at her feet. Even then she didn't look at him. He didn't want the gold. His share of it wasn't worth that much anyway. He said. "I don't want it. It's not that easy to shift that much gold without getting noticed." Shane got the suitcase and opened it under the light of the lamps. Rob said. "We would-n't have that either if it wasn't for me, it was my idea." Quietly Lola said. "I did the dirty work." Shane couldn't stand bickering, he said. "How much do you reckon?" Looking down at the open case, Rob rubbed his nose and thought for a moment. He said. "All I know is we had to leave some, I couldn't get it all in the case." Shane had seen the huge piles of cash that accumulated around Dennis and it didn't surprise him. Almost without moving, Lola gathered the rucksack to her and held it between her knees. Shane gave her a look, he said. "Empty that out of there. I want the bag."

Rob talked. It was part of his trade. It was part

of his cover. He was a natural born optimist. He had to be. He enjoyed ducking and diving, even though it sometimes backfired on him. But his optimism was at low tide. Lola hadn't listened to him at the times when it mattered most. If she had been prepared to share, they would all be on their way. Now he felt it was down to him to talk their way out of getting killed. He didn't care what he did or said. It was all bollocks anyway. He knew Shane didn't want to kill them. He'd known it ever since Shane had taken him into the toilet. If people want to hurt you they usually do. What he'd realized, even in Madrid, was that Shane didn't want to be to be noticed. He was unknown in Spain and he wanted it to remain that way. Shane did not want to be found. Not by Dennis or by the authorities. That was why he'd helped them when he could have walked away. That was why he'd agreed to kill the Cousin. Well, that and the money. And Lola too.

Trouble was Lola was stubborn. There wasn't a deal they could cut that would satisfy her. She didn't like to negotiate and took everyone for an idiot. But Rob, who only knew how to talk his way out of trouble or take his slaps, liked grey areas. He was a dealer and his nature was to negotiate. You gave him this, he gave you that. Violence didn't come into it with Rob. He could watch. He could take sides. He could be thankful it wasn't him. He could let fuckers like Shane beat on him and somehow rationalize it. Mostly he was like a rat in a corner. If he jumped he wasn't going for your throat but trying to jump over your shoulder. Survival had always been Rob's criterion. Had either Shane or Lola given him a few thousand quid and told him to fuck off, chances are he would now have taken the money.

He said. "Look, fuck it, see, I don't know how much is there, do I? Who could fucking know? Unless you're like that fucking autistic cunt or whatever the fuck in that film with Dustin fucking Hoffman and that Scientologist cunt. Face it right, most of us just can't do that shit. We are definitely two and two makes four but we ain't neurologically fucking wired to look at a fucking suitcase full of money and say, oh, one million pounds and twenty fucking P, sir." Rob's voice was beginning to grate so Shane smacked him one with the gun barrel across the forehead. Lola, who had begun to come back to life since she had the gold again, spat at Shane but it fell short. Shane said. "Empty the fucking bag." Clutching his forehead, Rob said. "It's too fucking easy!" Nobody argued. Rob said. "Hitting me, it's too fucking easy!" Shane said. "Shut up!"

Rob was sick of being discounted, like nothing he did or said was of any importance. His feelings hurt more than his forehead. He didn't shut up. He said. "You know what?" Shane didn't know what and he didn't care either. All he wanted to do was take the money and fuck off. In a snidey voice, Rob said "When we met in Madrid, that wasn't the first time we saw you. We saw you the night before too. Sitting right there at the same table. We thought you'd been sent to kill us. I checked you out, man. Walked past you three or four times but you didn't even see me. You only had eyes for the *señoritas*." Shane was beginning to get exasperated. He didn't need telling, he'd already figured out most of it. He said. "And?" With a smile for Rob, Lola decided to get in on the act and said. "Don't be a *limón*, Shane. The very next night, you see me." They were working in tandem again and that annoyed him. They were like flies buzzing around his eyes. What was the matter with them? Hadn't he already told Lola she could keep the gold? Rob said. "It wasn't an accident we met and you didn't come here thinking there was any fucking gold, did you?"

Now they were really getting on Shane's tits. He didn't want to hurt them but they were behaving like they had a death wish. Couldn't they see he was trying to be fair? He was squatting in front of the money trying to figure out how to carve it up and wondering if he should even bother. He looked at Lola hugging the bag of gold and Madrid seemed like a million years ago. She'd really smoozed him good and proper all the way and even now she'd kill him if she could. Yet despite everything, he still had a soft spot for her. One of the reasons he hadn't killed her was because she'd saved his life and fucked him all in minutes and he couldn't say that about many women. But Rob needed to shut the fuck up. Shane said. "No Rob, you're right, I didn't come here for the gold. I came here to fuck Lola." Waving the gun at Lola, he said. "Empty the bag and I'll be on my way." To Rob, he said. "I ain't going to kill you, either of you, unless you force me to. You should have told me about ripping Dennis off, though."

Rob wasn't listening. He was looking away into the night. He stood up and then as if to gain height, stood on the rock he'd been sitting on and stretched up on tippy-toe. Pointing, he said. "What's that?" Shane got to his feet and Lola stood up as well. A diffused white light was spreading through the treetops from somewhere below, back down the track and it was creeping slowly towards them. Now that they were listening they could hear the low growl of an engine.

This was what Shane didn't want. More people. He felt stupid for still being there. Felt stupid that Rob and Lola had conned him. That he'd allowed himself to be conned. He hated being stupid, hated it even more when he could see himself being stupid. Now was the time to go but he didn't. For a moment it was as though they were all hypnotized.

They didn't know what to do. Rob and Lola looked over their shoulders. Behind them was just a blackness made up of trees and mountains. It went on and on to nowhere either of them understood and they knew it. Lola said. "Fuck a duck! Bugger! Shit!" For the first time in a while, Rob smiled at Lola with affection and said. "You can be so fucking eloquent at times, my lovely." They looked at each other and back at the lights coming to get them.

Until he'd moved to Spain, Shane wouldn't have considered himself a loner. Now he wished he was on his own again. Back at his house stretched out on the couch, looking at the white walls and no fucker out there to bother him. It was like his mind had moved in the last four years and he hadn't even noticed. But the change was small. Shane still wanted excitement. He missed his buzz and he couldn't find a balance. There wasn't a release, for him, in normal life. Over the last few months it was like if he didn't keep his personality in check he'd kill someone, a stranger, a stupid fuck who just happened to get in his way. He didn't. He sublimated. That was what he'd been doing in Madrid. Adrenaline was like cocaine, it was vacuous. It didn't mean anything. He craved it though. It was like a power surge. It was his favourite buzz. You couldn't buy it, you could only do it. He'd had a taste again now and like all junkies his body craved more but he tried not to let it distract him.

He thought he knew exactly what he was doing but his need and loneliness had got him right here and he didn't much like it. He was out of practice and he knew it. The tussle with the Cousin had shown him that much. He couldn't even bring himself to kill Rob and Lola and he wasn't completely sure why. They annoyed him enough. Now they were both looking over at him like he would have some kind of a plan. He didn't. Shane's best idea was to disappear with the money, alone. He knew which way home was. All he had to do was find the ridge he was on earlier and follow it. By morning he would be well away and could find a road. His place was no more than fifty miles off, at the most. The lights were getting nearer. Rob said. "Shane?"

It was like everything was forgotten for them. Only nothing ever is, not really. Shane didn't bother to answer. He stooped down, dropped the lid and snapped shut the catches on the case. Too late to divvy-up, it was time to go. Lola still had the rucksack in one hand and before he could get fully to his feet, she swung it at his head. Shane ducked, grabbed her arm and dragging himself up to her level, hit her in the side of the face with the gun. Staggering, she sank to her knees and let out a loud sob. Maybe it was too much for Rob to see Lola hurt again or maybe he just had the urge to be heroic, whatever. In an ungainly looping movement he seemed to dive off the rock he was on and some-how grab up the shotgun from beside the tent. He'd almost managed to right himself before Shane kicked him in the head. The shotgun tumbled out of his hands. In desperation Lola tried to make a play for the fallen gun and Shane gave her another smack. This time when she fell she made sure the rucksack somehow ended up under her body. She hunkered over the gold, teeth bared, like she was ready to die rather than give it up.

Staying where he'd fallen, Rob held his head between his hands and groaned theatrically. Shane may have been out of practice but not for these two. He kicked Rob in the ribs and dragged Lola into a sitting position. Lola spat at him again. It landed on his crotch and dribbled off like waste spunk. Wrenching the rucksack from her, he put it with the suitcase. Still groaning, Rob pulled himself into a sitting position. He held his hands up, like a victim, he said. "Sorry, sorry. I don't know why the fuck I did that, it was stupid." Shane gave each a swift tolchock and a kick and said. "What the fuck is the matter with you two! Some fuckers are on their way up here! Do you want to get caught?" Rob said. "I just wanted to -. Fuck it man, I would-n't have known what to do with it anyway, even if you hadn't kicked me in the head. Fuck sake, can you see it? Me, shoot somebody?" Shane said. "Shut the fuck up!" Lola said. "Don't take the gold, please!" Still she wasn't begging, she was stating her claim. Shane said. "I told you to take the fucking gold out of the rucksack, you didn't." He hoisted the bag onto his back.

Someone's main beams were lighting up the trees and sky. He took the shotgun out of Rob's way and picked up the box of shells. Still holding the side of his head where Shane had kicked him, Rob scrambled to his feet. He said. "What you doing? Don't leave us!" He hopped around from foot to foot. He said. "No, no, look you got everything. You can have everything. You don't have to kill us. We won't tell anybody where you are. It'll be like you never existed. We'll just run off into the -." He hesitated and looked around. "I swear we won't -." Cracking open the gun and taking out the used cartridge, Shane pushed in a fresh shell and closed the breech. Rob stopped talking. They heard the vehicle drop a gear and grind up around the bend by the big rock.

Above their heads the lights shredded the forest and put it back together again before bouncing off the mountain behind them. Shane dropped the shotgun and shells into Lola's lap, he said. "You're going to need this." Rob said. "Who is it? Who's coming? Who? No, not more of Dennis's fucking mates! If we've got to kill all these people, what's the fucking money worth, like? They just keep coming. Fucksake! Fucksake! Can't we just go?

Can't we all just run off?" He looked from Shane to Lola. Lola rose to her feet. She had the gun in the crook of one arm as though she was born to hunt. Shane said. "You can do what you like." If Rob and Lola followed him he wouldn't stop them. He'd have to take the shotgun off Lola again alright but he wouldn't stop them. For some stupid reason he didn't want to see them die.

Stubborn to the end, Lola said. "You run away? The big man? The killer of all those poor policemen? Run away and take everything? You don't even want the gold. Leave us something. Leave me the gold. Leave me something to fight for." It was true, he didn't want the gold and he was only taking it because the pair of them had pissed him off so much. Like a toy worked by a remote button, Rob said. "She's right, man. Don't leave us with nothing after all this." Despite everything there was something about Lola's sheer jeezney that Shane liked. She hadn't given up, even now. She was actually ready to stand and fight. He slid the rucksack of his back, handed it to Rob and picked up the suitcase. After hoisting the bag onto his back, Rob smiled at Shane and was almost pathetic, when he said. "Don't go. Please." The light danced all blinding and white around them.

∽ 10 ∽

The vehicle's headlights cut every bush and rock short. Nothing around their little campsite was left unexposed. It was too late for anyone to go anywhere. Sure, they did the natural things. They backed off into the scrub, dropped to the ground and tried to take cover amongst the rocks and bushes. They got as close to the earth as possible, with no real idea whether they could be seen or not. There was only one vehicle but it was impossible to tell how many were inside. The engine idled for maybe a minute. So they lay there, waiting. There was nothing else to do. Like it mattered, Rob whispered. "Who the fuck is it?" Lola said. "Does it matter?" To Rob, Shane said. "Cops. Bet you it's that pair of *Guardia Civil* from the other evening." This seemed stranger to Rob than if it had been a cadre of Dennis's friends. His voice was a bit shaky when he said. "Cops? No? What do they want?"

In Rob's life the police didn't solve problems they only made things worse. They always thought they were in the right. But just because the law was on their side didn't mean they were right. He didn't like them. Unable to stop himself, he started to look around for a dark spot to run to but the car lights seemed to stretch all around them for ever. He knew the darkness was out the somewhere and now it didn't scare him half as much as it had earlier. The gold was on his back and for a moment he wondered if he was quick enough to find sanctuary out there, before some crazy Spanish cop shot him or worse. He said. "What if we run? What if we just fuck off right now, before they get out of the car?" Lola waved a hand at the campsite. "They know who I am already." Shane said. "And the two bodies in the BMW. We'd be public enemy number1. Fuck that. You do what you like. Now they're here, I'm going to kill the cunts." Rob knew exactly what Shane was capable of. He remembered the pictures in the newspapers of the dead cops spread all over the south London side street. It wasn't something you forgot. He lowered his head and lay the side of his face on the earth.

As if to settle him, Lola said. "Honey, they don't come here on police stuff, they are, as you would say, dodgy as fuck." Rob didn't care about that. He didn't have any more faith in the authorities than he had in the likes of Dennis or Shane. They were all sides of the same coin to Rob. Fuckers, one and all. Yet he would take Dennis or Shane over the law, anytime. He wished that they, whoever they were, would turn off the lights for just a moment and give him and Lola a chance. They did turn the engine off but left the lights on high beam.

Lola was lost, she wasn't thinking. To her this was like the last straw. She'd pushed herself out on a limb and the limb felt like it was breaking. And no matter what she had just said to Rob, if this was the police, then they knew and they were there because of her. Perhaps it had always only been a matter of time since Madrid. She didn't care. Not now. So much had happened life could never be the same again anyway. In the last few hours she had been taken so close to death she was beyond desperate. The shotgun lay cocked beside her.

Nothing had started. But something was coming. Stretched out in the dirt behind a rock not much bigger than an overgrown watermelon, Shane waited. Thin shadows cast by a scrub oak, a few feet in front of him, mottled his body like crap camouflage. The suitcase was beside him, touching his thigh. The automatic was in his hand. Shane readied himself. Everything about him tingled like he'd had the best of drugs. There was nothing like adrenalin. He had no idea what was going to happen. It made him want to smile.

Two men got out of the car. They were careful. Almost crouching behind the open doors, they spoke quietly to each other in Spanish. Rob hissed. "What they on about?" Shane whispered back. "Fuck knows but they ain't taking any chances." He couldn't figure it. Why would the *Guardia Civil* think they were dangerous? Did someone hear the shots and report it? No. Shane couldn't believe that. This was the *Campo*. People went hunting.

The driver shouted. "*Varela! Policía!*" Loudly, Lola yelled back. "*Putas!*" With a sigh, Rob tried to make himself flatter, more at one with the soil. The two men exchanged a few more words and began to chuckle. Again he shouted. "*Varela! Policía! Ríndete!* (Give yourself up!)" Lola spat back. "Fuck you!" The other mans giggle turned into a laugh and the driver shushed him. To Shane they both sounded a bit pissed. Once more the driver shouted, this time in fucked up English. "You English and you odour English. Come out. Come out now, please. No trouble. You accessorize only." After a few more hushed words between them, the other *Guardia* spoke up. His English was much better. He said. "We want to talk to *señorita Varela* about the murder of her aunt in Madrid. If you give yourselves up now it will go better for you." The driver, who Shane took to be the fatter, older cop, said loudly. "*Quizás!* (maybe!)"

Lola was quiet this time. Her hand wrapped itself around the shotgun's breach, a finger curled into the trigger guard. Rob and Shane were looking at her, they were both gobsmacked. She stared back at them. Rob said. "Fucking hell Lola!" She hissed, fiercely. "*Qué?* What? What!" Rob said. "You killed that old lady? What the fuck did you do that for?" Looking at Rob like he was some kind of congenital idiot, she said. "Honey, she irritated me. That bitch always made me feel foolish. As you say, fuck her." Looking across at Shane, Rob raised his eyebrows. Shane pulled a face and shrugged. The past was what had happened. He wasn't able to judge. Everything was personal. At least he now understood why the police were bothering with them. To the two men behind the car lights, he shouted, in Spanish. "*¿Cómo sabemos que sois policías? No siquiera podemos vemos. Muestranos algunas pruebas. Nos muestran una orden judicial o algún tipo de identificación.* (How do we know you're the cops? We can't even see you. Show us some proof. Show us a warrant or some kind of identification.)" Although Rob didn't understand what Shane had said, he yelled a follow up. "Yeh! Too fucking right!" Then he put his head back down in the dirt again and waited to be killed.

Two seconds passed and when he didn't die, he turned his face sideways so he could see Lola.

There was a look of concentration on her face. Nerves were darting down her jaw line. She was staring hard into the light, as though she could see through the glare to the two men. He didn't know how things had got so far out of control but he knew he loved Lola, knew that deep down he'd been lucky. She had chosen him. He didn't know why and he didn't try to understand why. He didn't care why. He'd had something, something special from a woman and even if it wasn't equal, it was the nearest to love he had ever been. The cops whispered amongst themselves and then the younger one, said, in English. "If you come forward -." Before he could finish the driver shouted him down. *"No tenemos qoe demostrar que no apesta insignias* (Fuck you! We don't have to show you no stinking badges!)" Rob said. "What's he on about now?" Shane pulled an uncomprehending face, he said. "Something about not having to show us no stinking badges."

Rob's mind went funny for a moment then, and he was back in the scuzzy council flat where he was dragged up. His mother was nodding out on the broken down couch and he was sat on the floor watching TV. A bunch of Mexican bandits were trying to cajole the prospectors from their hiding places. He said, to Shane or Lola or anyone. "That's what he said. What the bandit guy said to Humphrey Bogart. Fuck me. That's the famous line. I don't fucking believe it!" Neither Lola nor Shane really heard what he said, or if they did hear, cared. Lola shouted. "*Cabrones!* (Bastards!)" To the other two, Shane said. "We've got to do something. Get them to turn the lights out. We can't stay here. If they're cops on real cop business, then they're going to call for back up pretty soon." Lola sneered. "We'll kill them." Almost without hope, Rob begged, plaintively. "Lola" Shane said. "She's right. What else is there?"

None of them spoke for a little while. The cops were silent too. Rob said. "Let's try to bribe them." Reaching out Lola grasped his arm and said. "What with?" Prising her fingers from his arm, he said. "With what we've got." Lola tried to grab hold of him again but Rob dragged himself across the ground away from her. He shrugged the rucksack off his back and all the time Lola was grunting. "No, no, no." Rob started to undo the neck of the bag and turning on her side Lola tried to bring the shotgun around and level it at Rob. Shane was quicker. He pushed the barrel of his gun into the back of Lola's neck. He said. "Rob's right. These fuckers are a right couple of rubes. We gull them and then we'll kill them." Lola was careful now.

Almost without moving she put the gun back on the ground and without turning to look at Shane, said. "What are these rubes, this gull?" Shane said. "They're a couple of dumb shits, muppets. We trick them. We can't do anything laying here like this. We've got to get them out in the open." Rob took two of the gold bars out of the bag. To Lola, he said. "If you're going to murder them it doesn't matter what we give them does it? Anyway, what's the Spanish for treasure?" Lola didn't answer, so Shane said. "*Tesoro*." Under his breath, Rob repeated. "*Tesoro*, right?"

Rob stood up and waved his arms, He had a gold bar in each hand. He shouted. "*Tranquilo,tranquilo! Tesoro, tesoro!* Gold, gold!" From the ground, Shane said. "*Oro*." Rob looked down briefly and changed his cry. "*Oro,oro!*" He threw the gold bars one after the other towards the lights. They hit the car bonnet with a clatter and slid to the ground. Again Rob shouted. *Tesoro,tesoro! Oro, oro!*" He stood there unmoving in the glare of the lights like some stupid martyr without a cause. Nothing happened. If they had wanted to kill them, they would have started there and then with Rob. Shane said. "I think you've got their attention." Without looking down, Rob said. "I fucking hope so, I feel like a right twat standing up here."

There was conversation behind open doors. A black shadow came out all huddled down and began playing lost and found for one of the fallen bars. Maybe if Shane felt lucky he could have given it a shot but the whole night had been a little bit wrong somehow, a bit twisted and out of kilter. He waited and while he waited he kept an eye on Lola who was eyeing the rucksack like it was her child roasting on a spit. She was drooling but it was also her heart and soul. He poked her in a friendly fashion with the gun butt, he said. "Get it over here." Looking at him then, she almost smiled, before crabbing it to grab the gold. When the bag was beside her, Lola touched Shane on the hand that was holding the gun and quite suddenly for Shane, for the first time, they were all in it together.

In a low, slow drawl, Rob said. "Fucking dozy cunts. What's up with the toe wanking, cock socking, shoe licking, cunting twats. I bet their fucking wives or fucking little Maria bints are glad to see these hairy backed fucking burks leave for work in the morning. That's if the cunts could ever get themselves a fucking Maria bint in the first place. But then I've always thought that. I mean, like who would want to fuck a cop?" He giggled. Shane giggled. Lola pulled herself over to where he was standing and kissed his calf, just above the top of his sock" In the same droll tone, Rob continued. "These tosspots are like slow, know what I mean? Fucking retards on wobbly eggs. Didn't they ever see gold before or what? And I'm dying for a piss."

The main beams went to dip and then to sidelights but the two men stayed behind the protection of the open doors. For the first time it was possible to see the vehicle wasn't a police car but a rusty looking old pick-up. As though vindicated, Lola hissed. "See! They do not come as police." Shane said. "It doesn't matter, does it?" Rob said. "Just makes them easier to negotiate with." Pushing the handgun down the front of his jeans, Shane pulled his shirt over it and said. "Well, here goes." Getting to his knees, he scrambled upright and stood next to Rob. Under his breath, he said to Lola. "Leave the gun down there beside the gold and stand up." Lola squirmed. She didn't want to do it. It was her they were there for. She looked up at the two men, her eyes pleaded but slowly she rose to her feet and stood with them.

The gas lamps were still burning and with the faint light thrown by the pick-up's sidelights, the campsite was cast once more in a mellow glow. Still not taking any chances, the younger of the two cops called out, in English, for them to come forward. Shane looked at Lola and Rob. Lola was trembling. She looked profoundly unhappy. She sighed and under her breath, said "Bugger." Rob was shuffling his feet uncomfortably and looking around for a suitable spot to take a piss. He said. "It's getting fucking desperate, man." Shane said. "Just a couple more minutes. Wait until we've got them out into the open and talking." Rob said. "So you don't think they're going to kill us, then?" Lola said. "*Putas.*" Shane couldn't help glancing behind him at the suitcase, barely visible now in the dark. He wanted it but it didn't mean anything, not at this time. He just wanted something to happen. He said. "No, they could have done that any time. Fuck them, come on." Shane stepped forward and the other two followed.

They stood by the tent waiting. Little by little the two cops edged out from behind the open doors. They weren't dressed like *Guardia Civil* but like hunters. The older one had a flat cap pulled square on his head, a red and green checked shirt and heavy corduroy trousers tucked into calf high lace up boots. The young guy was in walking boots and denims. He had a dark woollen shirt underneath a sleeveless green jacket with appliqué leather pockets. Both men were carrying hunting rifles with telescopic sights. They came to the front of their pick-up, rifles held at their hips and pointing at Rob, Lola and Shane. Speaking out of the side of his mouth like a TV convict, Rob said. "These cunts look like they stepped straight out of a catalogue, you know, the page for manly pursuits."

The chubby cop came forward first. He had a sly, knowing grin on his face and stepping up to Lola poked her in the stomach with the barrel of the rifle. "*Señorita Varela. Nos reunimos de nuevo.* (Miss Varela. We meet again.)" From the top pocket of his shirt he took one of the gold ingots and waggled it in her face. "*Por lo tanto, un zorro puede oler su propio agujero, incluso después de todos*

*estos años. ¿Es por eso que usted mató a que la mala
vieja,eh? Su propia sangre, su Tia. Yo sabía que había
algo acerca de usted. Me corrió un cheque. La policía
de Madrid está buscando para usted y ahora tenemos,
no estamos señorita Varela.* (So a fox can still smell
its own hole even after all these years? Is this why
you killed that poor old woman, eh? Killed your
own blood, your own aunt! I knew there was something about you. I ran a check. Yes, the Police in
Madrid are looking for you, and now we have you,
don't we miss Varela.)" There was a slimy threat in
the way he dragged out the name Varela. Lola flared
her nostrils and spat in his face.

The ball of gob slid down the side of his nose and
on to his cheek. Maybe that was all he was waiting
for. His expression remained fixed around his grin
as he swiped at her and the edge of the gold ingot
in his hand caught her cheek hard and she staggered
a step back and fell to one knee. Lola held a hand
up to her face, her eyes all glittery and fixed like a
death star on the cop.

The younger one came forward now. He was
nervous, unsure. Keeping the other two covered, he
took a handkerchief from his pocket and handed it
to his partner, who, wiped away the sputum and
handed it back, his eyes locked on Lola the whole
time. Lola stayed where she was for the moment,
like she was ready to spring, lips tight back, teeth
bared. She took the hand away from her cheek.

There was a smear of blood on it and an ugly swollen weal down the side of her face. As she tried to stand up, the cop put the sole of his boot into her chest and sent her sprawling.

Lola came up as soon as she hit the ground and tried to throw herself at the short arse, portly dick. Shane grabbed her and held her and whispered in her ear. "Don't." Stepping back a pace, the two men brought their rifles up to their shoulders and Rob started hopping about from foot to foot and waving his arms and going. "*Tranquilo! Tranquilo!*" The men looked at each other nonplussed, not really recognizing their own language mangled by Rob's London accent. Still holding Lola, Shane said, in Spanish. "*No hay necesidad de violencia. Oro? Usted quiere una parte del ore? ¿Si? Entonces vamos a ser todos un poco más tranquilos, ¿eh?* (No need for violence. Gold. You want to share the gold? Yes? Then let us all be a little bit more friendly, eh?)" Pointing at the little gas burner, he said. "*Podriamos sentarnos, omar un café, hablar, negociar.* (We could sit down, have a coffee, talk, negotiate.)" He shrugged and smiled his most harmless smile. Rob was still dancing from foot to foot, except now he only had one hand in the air, like a school kid. The other was clutching his balls. To Shane he said. "Fuck this man, tell them! Tell them I got to take a slash! I draw the line at pissing myself." Shane couldn't help laughing a little bit. The cops said.

"*¿Qué?*(What?)" Shane said. "*Él necesita hacer un piss.*(He needs a piss.)" Somehow some of the tension went out of everything then and Shane let Lola go and the two cops laughed a little bit too.

11

The younger of the two men followed Rob the few yards to a bush and kept a watch over him as he pissed a small river. Shane lit the burner on the stove. Lola got the last saucepan out of the tent and filled it with water. The older cop, leery, watched every move she made as she bent to make more of her crap coffee. Shane could have taken him then. He didn't because the other one was too far away and Rob, with his prick in his mitt, wasn't going to be any help to anybody. As he relieved himself, he kept going. "Aaah, oooh, yyyes." It seemed to go on forever and so Shane smiled easy on the situation. Smiled on the cops and on Lola and on Rob and on anything that would ease the tension. He needed the *Guardia* off their guard, if only for a moment. When Rob had shaken the last drips from his dick and zippered himself up, he strolled back over to Shane and Lola like a new man.

Perky as fuck now, he rubbed his hands together and threw grins about like he had a sack full going spare. He said. "Thank fuck for that! What can you do when you want to piss? Nothing right! Can't think, can't drink, can't fuck but anyway, that's all water up a tree as they say, right?" He shuffled his shoulders up and down and shunted his hands and fore-arms back and forth like he was playing trains. "Now what are we going to do about my lovely Lola and this fucking gold, eh? Got to be something we can do, ain't there? Got to be a little give and take, know what I mean? Got to be a deal, what? Maybe we can all stroll away richer, eh?" It didn't matter how good their English was, the way Rob spoke was too quick and too London. The pair of them looked at each other and said nothing. They pulled faces and pretended they understood but it was bollocks.

Rob could see their confusion and it spurred him on. He started moving around, talking nonsense all the time. The two cops couldn't take their eyes off of his lanky figure as he pranced about getting cups and explaining that there was no milk or sugar and only three tin mugs. He was like an unknown species to them. For a few seconds their gun barrels dipped as they watched him and tried to make sense of his drivel. Then the older cop lost the plot and swung his rifle around and shouting for silence, smashed Rob in the chest with the butt. Rob staggered and tripping over a guy rope fell heavily to the ground, but he didn't shut up.

Up on his knees again, he rubbed his chest and said. "Fucksake geezer, no need for that! Just trying to be friendly, know what mean? *Amigos*, yeh?" The cop raised the butt again, but the young one grabbed his arm. Scrambling to his feet, Rob gave them a snide smile and as if to provoke them further, said. "That's it, *tranquilo, tranquilo,* yeh?" Chubby cursed and attempted to pull free but not too hard.

Anyway, the rifle barrels were up again. The five of them stood around looking at each other for a few moments, then the cops herded Shane, Lola and Rob to one side of the heating water and the five of them waited awkwardly, as though the coffee had some kind of significance. It didn't. Waving his gun around, Chubby said. "*¿Dónde está el oro?* (Where's the gold?)" Shane pointed behind him into the darkened scrub and grinned. Quietly to Rob and Lola, he said. "If they've got any sense they'll make one of us get it." Lola said. "Me, I go." Rob started to protest. "No lovely, no, I'll go."

Even if he couldn't understand him, the young one didn't want to hear any more of Rob's nonsense. Coming right up to him, he shouted in his face. "*Silenco tonto!* (silence fool)" It was too much for Rob who began to snigger and looked at Shane and it was too much for him too and then they were both giggling. Rob cocked a thumb at the cop and said. "What does that make you, The Lone fucking Ranger!" They both cackled even louder. Lola looked at them as nonplussed as the two *Guardia*.

The coffee boiled and Shane kicked out at the saucepan. The scalding water and grounds flew up into the air and instinctively the older man jumped back. A few spots landed on his trousers and that seemed to enrage him all over again. He jumped over the circle of rocks around the stove and shoved the business end of the barrel up against Shane's heart. Even on tippie-toe he only came up to the middle of Shane's chest but he had an evil eye. Shane didn't give a fuck. He grinned down on him and waited. Do it. Nothing happened. A cop's a cop however he's dressed and his evil eye was only a cop's evil eye. Under his breath, Shane said. "You're a dead motherfucker now." They looked at each other out of the corner of their eyes but neither of the *Guardia* understood a word. The young one took Rob by the arm and keeping Lola covered, pulled him away from Shane. He put Rob and Lola together and stood back off them like he'd read it in a textbook. Rob stuck his fingers up and gave Lola a kiss. Shane was actually beginning to like Rob.

Chubby pushed at Shane but Shane didn't go

anywhere. In his mangled English, Chubby said. "You, get gold." Shane grinned some more and shook his head. He didn't like looking down on people but with some people you couldn't help it. Lola started then. *"Espere, espere, voy a ir. Me pondré por ti. Por favor, no más. Un momento por favor espere, voy conseguilo.* (Wait, wait, I'll go. I'll get it for you. One moment, wait please, I'll get it.)" She didn't wait for permission. She turned away and started to walk into the scrub. Chubby's eyes were everywhere then and he stood back from Shane and motioned to Rob and said. *"Usted, tonto, aquí!* (You, fool, over here!)" Rob gave a little laugh and said. "Right on Kemo Sabe." To his mate, Chubby said. *"Vigila de cerca a ella.* (Keep a watch on her.)"

The young *Guardia* moved towards the darker area beyond the weak lights of the campsite and the older man stood well off Shane and Rob, as he tried to keep an eye on his friend. Nobody had to wait long. The report of the hunting rifle was loud and sharp and it was followed instantly by the double blast of the shotgun. The young man seemed to flip back into sight like an acrobat and a cloud of dust ballooned up as the body landed. His chest and abdomen were ripped open but he wasn't quite dead and lay there twitching in the lambent light. Chubby was too shocked and too slow and Shane shoulder charged him. They went down scrabbling but there was no real fight. Shane ripped the rifle from his hands and smashed the butt into his face a few times. The cop's nose and cheekbones smashed and he gurgled and screamed. Throwing the rifle to one side, Shane pulled the gun out from under his shirt and smiling down into the man's blooded eyes, shot him through the forehead.

12

By the time Shane had his man on the ground, Rob was already running. He jumped the twitching, eviscerated man dying in the dust and a few yards further on, fell to his knees over Lola's stricken body. The bullet had hit her in the neck, opening up her jugular and tearing a ragged hole out through the other side. Her head seemed to be pillowed in a great, gathering, dark pool. Blood pumped lethargically from the wide open vein and Rob tore off the sleeveless puffa jacket he wore, tossed it to one side and pulled his T shirt over his head and tried to staunch the flow. Lola wasn't dead but she would be soon. Rob started to cry. He held her shoulders in his hands and rested his forehead on hers. He said. "My lovely, my beauty, my darling." Lola couldn't hear him. She was breathing but it was last knockings. He kissed her cheeks and kissed away the blood bubbling out from between her lips. He held his mouth against hers until after the last breath had left Lola's body. He stayed hunched over her like that, letting the tears flow. He heard the pathetic low key moans from the dying cop behind him and he heard the loud report from Shane's gun. Nothing mattered to Rob in those moments. Nothing.

Shane stood up and stuck the gun back into the waistband of his jeans. He looked down on the man he'd killed and gave the corpse a kick. He hadn't like the fucker from the moment they'd met in the car park at the bottom of the track. The feeling, he guessed, had been mutual. He went through the dead man's pockets. There was about thirty quid in Pesetas, a driving licence and some other bits of ID. Shane put the cash in his pocket and threw the rest onto the dead man's chest. The night was starting to go grey and somewhere far away the sun was rising. He looked around and sighed. Everything was different now.

Before, when Shane had kicked out at the saucepan the little stove had fallen over and kept on burning. The grass around it was done to a crisp. He bent, righted the stove and turned off the gas. He walked over and looked down at the dying young man. Half of his guts were hanging out in dirty black and purple coils. His chest was ripped open but somehow he was still breathing, after a fashion. His eyes were closed. His body convulsed in tiny little spasms every few seconds. One of his hands still held the hunting rifle. Shane stepped around him and over to Rob.

When Shane put his hand on Rob's shoulder, Rob turned his head slowly and looked at him with big see-nothing eyes. Shane said. "Dead?" Rob nodded. For once in his life he didn't have anything to say. Neither did Shane. Everything would have been quiet if it hadn't been for matey and his groans. Shane took the gun out again and said. "Do you want to kill him?" Pulling a horrible face full of pain, Rob shook his head. After a moment, he said. "I never wanted to kill anybody." It was no good Shane trying to tell Rob that he didn't want to do it either, so he squeezed his shoulder and went over and put the young cop out of his misery.

It wasn't any good either, attempting to tell Rob he was wasting his time moving Lola. Instead, when he saw Rob struggling with Lola's body, he offered to help. Rob shook his head and got shakily to his feet, Lola clasped against his chest. Back by the tent Rob was like a man in a trance. He stood looking about, not knowing what to do next. Shane said. "Why don't you lay her down in the tent?" Rob lifted his chin and nodded a couple of little nods in Shane's direction. Shane pulled back the tent flaps and with a bit of effort, Rob managed to manoeuvre Lola's body inside. Shane dropped the flaps and went over to Chubby and gave him another couple of kicks. Fuck him.

There is only so long you can grieve and every situation is different. Shane sat on a rock and waited. Things were starting to get light all around and little birds were starting to sing and even fly about. It was going to be another perfect day in Extremadura. Something had to happen, so Shane went over to the tent and rustled the flaps. Rob came out as white as a ghost. His face was still twisted with pain but he said, by way of explanation. "She was never going to give up that gold once she'd got it." Shane didn't know what came over him but he opened up his arms and welcomed Rob in. They stood there like that hugging each other and Shane didn't even really mind that Rob cried on his shoulder.

It was Rob who pulled away first and rubbed his eyes and said. "Fucksake, it's morning." He looked behind him at the tent and back to Shane, he said. "She was a dingbat but I loved her." Shane took hold of Rob again then and held him and said in his ear. "I know, I know." Even though he didn't know.

Something had to be done. In the end dead people don't mean fuck all. They ain't the people you knew and loved or even hated. They are dead meat and if you were hungry enough you'd eat them. Shane said. "We have to leave or we're fucked."

Shane took out the clothes he'd put in the bag with his tent. He didn't like to do it but he asked Rob to go back and bring out the clothes from their tent as well. Rob was well enough to walk at least and after a little while he came back out with some stuff. As Rob was walking Shane thought it would do him good, so he kept him scuttling about. Next he asked him to bring over the suitcase of money and the rucksack of gold. Then he made him find the two bars of gold he'd thrown at the cops. That took a little bit of time, as one bar was in one of the patch pockets of the young cops hunting waistcoat and the other was in the dust next to Chubby's corpse. Rob didn't know why he did what Shane told him and he was to numb to care. He moved because he was alive.

While Rob was going about his tasks, Shane got busy. He took all the clothes over to the BMW. The saucepan had overflowed a while ago and the ground under the petrol tank was wet with it. He took the full saucepan out from under the car and poured it all over the clothes and shoved them under the petrol tank. Then carefully, he got the saucepan and getting his head and shoulders under the car, pushed the saucepan between the bundle of clothes and the petrol tank. He fiddled around a bit until he was sure he'd got the plink, plink of petrol into the saucepan. He left a tail of petrol wet clothes hanging out from under the car.

Shane went back over to Rob then and had a look at him. There were smears of Lola's blood on his chest and face. His eyes still had that space cadet look in them. He wasn't talking much. Shane got the water and gave him a rough wash and put a T shirt and a jumper on him. He went through Rob's pockets until he found his little pill case. There were three pills left. Shane held them out to Rob and shrugged. They had to walk out of there and it had been a long night. Rob took one. Shane took one. Rob split the last one between the nails of his thumb and forefinger and they each had a cheeky half. Shane made sure Rob had got all his papers and anything that had anything to do with him. But by the time they were getting ready to leave, Rob was already coming back to himself. As they transferred the gold from Shane's rucksack into Rob's and the money from the suitcase into Shane's bag, he said. "She wouldn't have liked being burned but being cremated is different, right?" Then he laughed.

The last thing they had to do was get the Cousin and his mate out of the boot. Rob didn't want to do it at first but Shane didn't want to argue. It was hard for them both and the Cousin was double heavy dead. Shane wished for Lola rather than Rob as a help mate. They dragged the corpses out of the boot, let them fall to the ground and pulled them to somewhere between the cars and the tent. Shane didn't bother to explain to Rob, all he said was. "That's it, let's get gone."

Shane took the rucksack with the cash in it and Rob carried the one with the gold. They followed the path Shane had found the day before, up onto the ridge. Shane left Rob there then and went back down to the camp site. He took the petrol caps off the pick-up and the 4x4. He got the stove and taking it over to the BMW, put a lighter to the gas, placed the stove down against the petrol soaked tail coming out from under the car, and stepped back. A blue flame wavered up off the petrol soaked cloth and began to creep towards the BMW's undercarriage. Shane went back up the path to Rob.

They walked along the ridge for about ten minutes, the pleasant morning sun coming down on them through the high trees and the E buzz coming up on them and giving them both some fresh energy. They heard the WUMPH as the first car went up and they could see the spiralling cloud of dirty grey smoke up in the sky. They started to move faster. Less then ten minutes later there was a second explosion and not long after that, a third. The cloud of smoke was now huge, greasy and black and shot through with bright orange flames.

Mostly they hiked in silence. There wasn't anything to say. At one point, Rob stopped and turned to look at the fire gathering pace at their backs. He said. "You don't think it'll catch us, do you?" Shane said. "I hope not." Rob said. "How do you think they put things like that out?" Shane shrugged. "Fuck knows." Rob said. "In the South of France they have these planes that scoop up great loads of sea water and then dump it on the fires." Shane said. "Where did you see that, on day-time telly?" Rob said. "How did you guess?" He pulled a face and said. "One year they found the remains of a scuba diver in the ashes." They both almost laughed. Rob said. "How fucking unlucky is that, eh?" They walked on. After another couple of miles they found a trail leading down to a road. The path came off the other side of the ridge onto a nar-row black top. As they came onto the road, Rob looked back up the path and shook his head. He said. "The countryside is weird ain't it? It's like it's all the same. It's just fucking trees and shit." They kept walking.

∾ 13 ∾

It took three or four hours walking before they came across another one of those half arsed, half dead, Spanish towns. By then they were fucked, dehydrated, hungry and over exposed to the sun. Some optimist had built a big modern bar on the town's outskirts. It had a restaurant full of plastic furniture and rooms to rent above. They sat at the bar and drank beer and ate some of every *tapa* that was on offer. The drugs were draining out of their systems now and both men were incredibly weary. Shane booked them a double room but they still sat at the bar for a while, unwilling for whatever reason to go immediately to sleep.

Rob was feeling maudlin, so they drank a couple of whiskies. Rob said. "I know I called her a dingbat but she wasn't crazy. She - she was determined, you know? Fucking determined. She kind off dragged me along with her. She was right, if it wasn't for her, I'd still be working for Dennis." Shane didn't know what to do or say. He patted Rob's back and said. "You're daft as a brush you know that, don't you?" With a shrug, Rob said. "Maybe, but you can't help who you love can you? I loved her." Shane did his best to be sympathetic, he said. "Well you two had something going, didn't you?" He ordered more drink. Rob said. "We had something alright. Don't know what it was exactly. I loved her but fuck it, I knew she'd dump me sooner or later."

Shane thought he'd try and change the subject, he said. "It ain't all bad. You got the gold and you're still alive." Rob held up his whisky and they clinked glasses. Still he didn't look happy. Shane said. "Okay, tell me, what made you go up and look around that rock for the gold?" At last Rob came up with a real smile. He downed his drink and signalled to the barman for two more, he said. "It was fucking obvious. That fucking great rock was the only thing in the picture you could really see." Shane shook his head and laughed, he said. "You ain't that fucking daft, are you!"

They sat in silence and drank for a bit. After a while, Rob said. "I know you and Lola - well, you know." He wasn't accusing Shane, it was just a statement. Shane said. "Did you see us?" Rob shook his head. "No. I didn't need to. A lot of people wanted Lola." Shane said. "Dennis?" Rob said. "Yeh. He'd been after her on the quiet for a while. I knew all Dennis's runnin's, you know? Knew where the money was, knew when it was there. Fuck it, I'd been working for him for long enough, right? Anyway, Lola went to see him. She left a window open for me. It was easy."

They slept until ten that night and when they went back down to the bar to eat, the local talk was all about the forest fire. Shane told the owner, it was a shame because that was where they were heading next. In the morning they got a Taxi to another town and a Taxi from there to yet another town and a Taxi from there to Shane's house. Shane let Rob stay for a week and then arranged for Jesus to go with him to Morocco.

Six weeks later the phone rang. It was Dennis. Shane said. "How did you find me?" Dennis laughed, he said. "I've always known where you were."

fiction direct

If you enjoyed any of the **Shane** series, or would like to make any comments or have any enquiries regarding **Fiction Direct**, please e-mail **Fiction Direct** at:

info@fictiondirect.com

Coming Soon

SHANE BIT'D

WHERE DOES THE FUTURE START?

The first time you win a playground fight?
The first time your father takes you out robbing?
The first time you realize that nothing
really matters?
The first time everything becomes a weapon?

The first time?

No.

It's years later.

That's when the shit really hits the fan.